DURYODHANA

DURYODHANA

The Other Side Of The Mahabharata

NIVASINI

To my sister—
The moon to my tides,
The wind to my wings,
The voice that always said,
"Keep going."

And so I did.

ACKNOWLEDGEMENTS

To my parents—
The hands that held me steady,
The hearts that beat with mine,
The quiet strength behind every word.

To my English teachers—
Who lit the fire of stories within me,
Who taught me that words are not just written,
But felt.

To my friends—
The laughter in my storms,
The voices that silenced my doubts,
The unwavering light in my journey.

And to you, dear readers—
for breathing life into these pages,
For giving my words a home.

TABLE OF CONTENTS

AUTHOR'S NOTE

The Mahabharata is one of the greatest epics ever told—

a story of war, fate, and dharma that has shaped the cultural and moral fabric of generations. It is a tale often told from the perspective of the victors, painting a clear distinction between the righteous and the fallen. But history, as we know, is never truly one-sided.

This book is an attempt to revisit the Mahabharata through the eyes of Duryodhana—the man history remembers as the greatest villain of the epic. But was he only that? Was he purely evil, or was he a prince born into a world that had already decided his fate? This narrative ***does not seek to justify his actions*** but to explore the nuances of his choices, his relationships, and the burdens he carried. This is a work of ***mythological fiction***, ***not a historical or religious account***.

While inspired by the Mahabharata, it presents a ***fictionalized perspective*** on Duryodhana's story.

It re-examines the concept of dharma, breaking away from the simple binary of good versus evil, and instead embraces the complexity of human nature.

It is important to note that this book is purely a retelling from ***Duryodhana's perspective***.

His thoughts, emotions, and justifications are his own, shaped by his understanding of the world around him.

This ***does not*** reflect _my personal beliefs or interpretations_ of the Mahabharata.

Rather, it is an exercise in storytelling—an exploration of a voice often unheard, a perspective often dismissed.

The Mahabharata, at its core, is a story of choices. And in every story, the villain believes himself to be the hero. Perhaps, in this version, you may see why.

PROLOGUE

The battlefield is silent.

Kurukshetra, once alive with the roar of war, now lies beneath a shroud of death. The soil, soaked in the blood of warriors, drinks deeply, erasing the last traces of their existence. The cries of my brothers, my allies, my people—all are gone. I, too, have fallen. My body broken, my strength lost.

But my story is not over.

I stand now in a realm beyond life, before the unyielding gaze of Yama, the lord of justice. His presence is vast, stretching beyond time, his judgment absolute. Around me, shadows stir, whispering the fate that awaits me. I know what they expect.

That I will be condemned.

That my soul will be cast into darkness for my arrogance, my ambition, my defiance.

For the world, I am the villain. The tyrant. The man who brought ruin upon himself and his kin.

But I have spent a lifetime being judged by those who never sought to understand me. The world remembers what is convenient, what aligns with the narrative of the victors. But the truth is never so simple.

Right and wrong are never so clear.

I lift my head and meet Yama's gaze.

"Before you pass judgment," I say, my voice unwavering, "hear my side. You have heard the victors. You have heard the righteous. Now, listen to the man they call Duryodhana."

For the first time, the god of justice hesitates. The shadows still.

And so, I begin.

Not seeking mercy. Not pleading for absolution.

Only for the right to be heard.

History remembers victors as heroes and their rivals as villains, but I, Duryodhana, the son of Dhritarashtra, will tell you the truth—the truth of a man who fought not for power, but for justice in a world that refused to see it.

Chapter 1
✦ THE BEGINNING ✦

In the halls of Hastinapur, where duty and destiny collided, I was branded a villain. But before you judge me, hear my truth—the truth of a prince who was never meant to be a king, but fought for a crown nonetheless.

I was born into a world where the light of the throne was always just out of reach, a shadow cast long before my first breath. My father, Dhritarashtra, blind to the world in more ways than one, could not see the truth of what I was. And yet, I knew my destiny would not be defined by his failures, nor by the grandeur that was promised to my cousins.

The kingdom, the throne—it was never a gift. It was a battle I was forced to fight.

They call me jealous, cruel, power-hungry. Perhaps I am, but only because I saw the world as it truly was—a place where no one would give me what was rightfully mine unless I took it with my own hands.

I never wanted to be the villain of the story, but I was never given the chance to be anything else. I was not born to be the noble hero, nor was I the obedient son. I was the son of a king who could never truly rule, and in that, I found my own path.

As a child, I never knew light. The light I speak of was not the sun's warmth or the candle that flickered at the palace's grand hall—no, it was the light of power, of a future that never belonged to me.

My father- *he was a king without a throne, a ruler without vision.* And I, his son, was the heir to a kingdom I could never inherit.

In those early years, it was the faces of others that shaped me—the faces of my cousins, the Pandavas, who had the fortune of being born to a mother who was adored, and a father who was revered. I was the son of Dhritarashtra, and that alone branded me as lesser. *For what worth is a blind king's son?* I was an afterthought, a whisper in the corridors of power.

My earliest memories are of watching my mother, Gandhari, weeping in silence. Her tears were not for the fate of her own children but for the fate of my father's legacy, a legacy that would be inherited by men who could never truly understand what it meant to fight for a place at the table.

My brothers and I, born into this world of silence and shadows, knew that our father could not protect us. I learned, very early on, that nothing is given freely. **Power must be seized.**

My bond with Karna was my first taste of kinship.

When I was a boy, Karna and I shared more than just the frustration of being overlooked—we shared a sense of injustice that boiled beneath our skin.

He, an untouchable, a son of a charioteer; I, the son of a blind king. He was cast aside by the world for his birth, and I was seen as weak for mine. But together, we forged a friendship—one that ran deeper than the blood ties that bound me to the Pandavas.

In Karna, I saw something that no one else could see. **Strength.** Not just physical strength, but the kind of strength that comes from defying the world's expectations, from fighting every day just to be seen, just to matter.

I admired him for his courage and his refusal to bow to anyone— even when the world turned its back on him.

He was my *brother in spirit*, if not by blood. In those early days, it was Karna's presence that made me feel like I was not alone.

The Pandavas, however, were always in the light.

Yudhishtira was the *perfect son*. He had everything: wisdom, grace, and the approval of every elder in the court.

Bhima was a force of nature, *brash and loud*, with no thought for anything but his own strength.

Arjuna was the *darling of the women and the men alike*. His bow never missed its mark, and his heart never wavered. Nakula and Sahadeva, *twin shadows in their own right*, were quietly perfect in their own ways.

To the kingdom, they were the hope, the pride, the future. But to me, they were **the others**. The ones who belonged, while I stood outside, forever seeking my place.

There was always a distance between us. Not just in age, but in the way the world looked at us.

To them, I was the son of the blind king, a shadow destined to fade. They were the sons of the rightful king, the light destined to lead.

Even the elders, like Bhishma, who had sworn to protect Hastinapur, looked at me with pity.

Their eyes saw my potential as a threat, and they treated me like one. But the deeper they pushed me, the harder I fought back.

At those moments, I learned what it meant to be overlooked. And that is where the seed of bitterness began to grow.

The day I swore to take what was mine was not one of rage but of clarity.

It came slowly, like the dawning of the sun after years of darkness. The day I first looked at the throne and understood that it would never be mine unless I took it. My cousins—***my brothers***, I thought of them at the time—had the world handed to them on a silver platter, while I was left with nothing.

And for all the wisdom they spoke of, for all the lessons of dharma they followed, I could not help but feel the truth of the world in my bones: **In this world, power is never given. It is seized.**

I did not wish to be hated. I did not wish for the enmity that followed me, but as I stood in the courtyard that day, watching my father's unseeing eyes meet my gaze, I understood that I would never be accepted by the world as I was. So I would change the world.

That was the beginning of the end.

But how could they understand? How could they understand a prince who fought not for pride, not for vengeance, but for something far deeper—a place to belong, a right to sit where the light could touch him? I was not born to be the villain. ***I was born to be a king.***

I swore that day, alone in the silent halls of the palace, that I would rise, even if I had to rise from the ashes of the world that had forgotten me.

And I would do it with Karna by my side, because in him, I saw the one true ally who understood that the world would never give us a seat at its table—**we would have to take it ourselves.**

Chapter 2
✦ECHOES OF THE KURU THRONE✦

The Kuru Palace was a grand edifice, filled with opulence and riches beyond measure. But to me, it was more a gilded cage than a home. The towering columns and intricately carved walls may have dazzled the eyes of visitors, but all I could see were the walls that separated me from my destiny. My father sat on a throne that never truly held him. In those early days, I often wondered if I, too, would end up blind—not in my eyes, but in my heart, **just like him.**

From the moment I could walk, I knew something was wrong. The throne was not meant for me. I could feel it in the way the courtiers looked at me as if I was a shadow rather than a prince.

They spoke of my birth as if it was a *mistake*, the result of a marriage forced by the duty of kingship.

He loved me, of course, but his love was blind. His affection never translated into guidance or strength. He was a king without sight—both literal and figurative.

And I was his son, the heir to a throne that had no meaning in my hands. **What good is a throne that you cannot sit on? What good is power that you cannot wield?**

I was constantly measured against the Pandavas, always compared to their virtues, their strengths, and their favor with the elders.

Yudhishtira was the *ideal son*, the one who could do no wrong in the eyes of the people. His wisdom, his calm demeanor, his ability to hold the reins of responsibility—he was everything I was not. He was the *future king*, the one the people loved, the one they expected to lead. Every time I looked at him, I saw not a brother but a rival, a reflection of everything I was *supposed* to be.

Then there was Bhima—his strength was legendary, but it was also his weakness. He didn't think, didn't plan; his strength was a weapon of brute force, and the world seemed to adore him for it. I hated him, not because of his might, but because of the ease with which he *received everything*. Bhima never had to earn the affection of our father. Bhima never had to prove himself. His strength alone was enough.

Arjuna—*he*, who was revered above all for his archery, whose bow could split the heavens, who was adored by every woman in the palace, who had the favor of the gods. I envied him most of all, not for his skill but for the natural love he received from those around him.

His every victory seemed preordained, his every word cherished.

Even in the eyes of *Krishna*, Arjuna was the favored one, the chosen hero.

And then there were the twins, Nakula and Sahadeva—always so perfect, so quiet, so obedient.

They did not take after their father, but they were loved simply for their grace, their humility, and their good nature. To them, life was easy. To me, it was a constant struggle to be seen, to be heard, to matter.

But no one saw what I saw. No one understood that the weight of the world had been placed on my shoulders from the moment I took my first breath.

In those early years, I realized that if I was ever to sit on the throne, I would have to fight for it. No one would hand it to me. No one would give it to me because I was a son of a blind king. **I was already cast in the role of the villain before I had even made my first move.**

If my father's blindness was a curse, then the elders of Hastinapura were the chains that bound me. They were the ones who whispered behind closed doors, who spoke of me as if I were a threat rather than an heir, who looked upon my every action with suspicion.

Bhishma was the worst of them all. He who had sworn an oath to protect the throne—how could he protect me when his eyes were constantly focused on the Pandavas, constantly weighing their worth against mine?

He gave me no love, no encouragement, just sharp looks that felt like daggers every time I faltered.

His favoritism toward the Pandavas was as clear as the sunlight, but he was blind to the injustice it caused me.

I knew then that no one would help me. No one would stand by my side when the time came to take what was rightfully mine. It was all a game to them—**a game where I was never meant to win.**

But that was the moment I understood that I could not rely on anyone but myself. The palace, with its grand corridors and endless courtyards, became a place of cold walls and silent eyes. I realized that to gain what I was owed—what I had been born to—**I would have to make my own path.**

I watched my cousins with quiet resentment. They had everything that I had been denied. They had love, they had attention, and they had the favor of the elders.

And they took it all for granted. But I, would not take anything for granted.

I would make them see me. I would make them acknowledge that I was just as worthy, just as capable, as any of them.

I made a promise to myself that no matter what happened, *I would rise.* Not just because of my birthright, but because I knew, deep down, that the world would never give me what I wanted unless I took it by force. **If they could not see my worth, I would make them see it.**

Chapter 3
✦THE FRACTURED BROTHERHOOD✦

They call them my cousins.

They call them *my brothers*.

But to me, the Pandavas have always been the barrier standing between me and everything I was born to claim. My rivalry with them was not born from hatred—*it grew*, like a weed in the cracks of a stone, nourished by years of favoritism, humiliation, and the whispers of elders who never saw me as their equal. They were the golden sons of Hastinapura, and I was the shadow they cast behind them.

From the moment I could understand the word "Dharma," it was tied to Yudhishtira's name. The elders praised him endlessly for his wisdom, his calmness, and his fairness. "The rightful king," they would call him.

"A true Kuru."

But what made him more deserving than me? His birth? His calm demeanor?

His blind devotion to rules he barely understood?

The truth is, Yudhishtira was never a threat to me because of his virtues. He was a threat because of the narrative the world built around him. He didn't have to fight for anything. The world handed him loyalty, love, and trust, while I had to claw for even a moment's acknowledgment.

What angered me most was his arrogance cloaked in humility. He always spoke to me with gentle words, as if he pitied me. His tone was calm, almost fatherly, as though he believed he was my better in every way. It infuriated me. How could a man who never lifted a finger to fight for his place assume he was destined to rule?

I, who had fought for every scrap of respect I'd earned, **would never bow to a man like Yudhishtira.**

If Yudhishtira's quiet arrogance infuriated me, Bhima's open disdain cut me to my core. As children, Bhima's favorite pastime was humiliating me. He would shove me into the mud, laugh as I struggled to lift a mace, and challenge me to feats of strength he knew I could never win.

I still remember the day he pushed me into a pond in front of the palace courtiers. The laughter that erupted from the crowd that day still echoes in my ears. Bhima's strength was his weapon, and he wielded it without mercy.

To him, I was nothing more than a toy, a punching bag to prove his superiority. And the worst part? *No one stopped him.*

Bhishma, Vidura, and even my father turned a blind eye to his actions, dismissing them as childish pranks. But they weren't pranks to me. They were lessons.

Lessons that taught me the world would always side with the strong, and if I wanted to survive, I would have to become stronger than Bhima.

It was Bhima who made me pick up the mace for the first time.

Not out of love for the weapon, but out of the sheer desire to one day beat him at his own game.

Every time I trained, every swing of the mace, every bead of sweat on my brow—it was all for the day I would see the look on Bhima's face **when I finally bested him.**

If Bhima's strength was a constant reminder of my struggles, Arjuna's skill was a dagger to my pride. He was the favorite of everyone—Krishna, the gods, the teachers, the people. He excelled in everything he touched, from archery to combat, and he did it with an ease that infuriated me.

Arjuna was the kind of man who could charm the crowd simply by existing.

His victories were celebrated as *divine will*, and his failures were dismissed as *destiny's test*.

To the world, he was the epitome of what a warrior should be.

To me, he was a man who had never known the sting of being overlooked, the pain of fighting for recognition.

Our rivalry was inevitable. Every competition we entered turned into a battle of wills. I fought not just to win, but to prove that I was just as capable, just as worthy. But no matter how hard I tried, the world refused to see me. Even when I bested him in combat, the praise was hollow, the admiration fleeting. Arjuna didn't just outshine me—**he eclipsed me**, leaving me struggling in his shadow.

Nakula and Sahadeva were never as openly antagonistic as Bhima or as celebrated as Arjuna, but their mere presence was a reminder of the Pandavas' perfection.

They were graceful, obedient, and flawless in their own quiet way. *Their humility was maddening.*

It wasn't that they sought to challenge me, but their existence reinforced the idea that the Pandavas were untouchable, a force I could never defeat.

They were the calm to my storm, the balance to my rage, and it infuriated me. They didn't need to raise their voices or their weapons to prove their superiority—it was inherent, **a birthright they carried effortlessly.**

Our childhood was not filled with brotherly love but with constant competition. Every game in the palace courtyard, and every lesson in the guru's ashram, turned into a battle of egos.

The elders may have called it a harmless rivalry, but to me, *it was war.*

A war for respect, for recognition, for a place in a world that seemed designed to exclude me.

One particular memory stands out—the day of the archery contest. Dronacharya had set up a wooden bird as the target, challenging each of us to hit its eye. Yudhishtira was calm and composed but missed his mark. Bhima, strong and reckless, barely hit the bird. But then came Arjuna, who struck the eye with effortless precision. The applause that followed was deafening, and the look of pride on Dronacharya's face was unbearable.

When it was my turn, the silence was heavier than the bow in my hands.

I missed.

I didn't even come close. The laughter that followed was subtle and polite, but it cut deeper than any insult.

I realized that no matter how hard I tried, I would always be seen as *second to the Pandavas*.

It was not the first time I had seen favoritism in the name of dharma, nor would it be the last. But this one remained etched in my memory, a lesson in how power shields its own.

The gurukul grounds had never been silent, not with the clang of weapons, the sharp exhalations of sparring warriors, and the weight of commands from Dronacharya.

But that day, the silence was unbearable.

Ekalavya stood in the middle of the training grounds, his right thumb severed, blood dripping onto the soil beneath him. His face did not betray pain, only a quiet acceptance. His skill was unmatched, yet it had cost him the very weapon that had made him formidable.

And Dronacharya stood before him, holding that severed thumb as if it were some sacred offering.

I clenched my fists. This was not justice.

I remember how it had all begun—not with Dronacharya, not even with Ekalavya, but with Arjuna.

It was Arjuna who had first seen the Nishada prince practicing in the forest, standing before a crude clay image of Dronacharya, drawing his bowstring with a grace that even we had not yet mastered. Arjuna had returned to the gurukul troubled, his voice tight with concern as he told acharya what he had witnessed. Concerned, not awed—because he knew, even then, that Ekalavya was not just good, but better.

And Dronacharya had listened.

Ekalavya had surpassed all of us—**even Arjuna.** Everyone had seen it.

A boy with no royal lineage, no privilege, no access to the finest masters had outdone the so-called greatest disciple of Dronacharya. And for that, he had been punished.

I could not hold back any longer. "Acharya..." I called out, stepping forward, "was this his crime? That he was better than Arjuna?"

A murmur spread among the assembled students. Arjuna stiffened.

Dronacharya did not turn to face me, his gaze still fixed upon Ekalavya, who now bowed before him—a boy who had given up his very essence in devotion to his guru.

I laughed bitterly. "How fortunate Arjuna is, to have a teacher who removes every obstacle in his path! A teacher who ensures that no one—no matter how skilled—can outshine him."

Dronacharya's eyes finally met mine. There was no anger in them, only a deep, unwavering conviction. "Duryodhana," he said, his voice calm, "loyalty is worth more than skill. Arjuna is my disciple, bound to me by duty and allegiance. Ekalavya was not."

I scoffed. "Not because he didn't want to be—but because you refused him!"

Dronacharya remained silent, his face unreadable.

I turned to Arjuna, who stood still, the weight of his master's favor resting heavily upon him. Did he not see it? Did he not see how the path had been cleared for him at the cost of another's future?

Ekalavya had not needed Dronacharya's presence, nor his guidance—he had needed only inspiration.

And that was enough for him to master the art that we all struggled to perfect.

And yet, his reward was ruin.

I turned back to Dronacharya, my voice steady but filled with contempt. "This is not teaching. This is not dharma. This is ensuring that power remains where it has always been."

And for the first time, I saw it—the flicker of guilt in my guru's eyes.

The Pandavas were not just my rivals—they were my greatest challenge, my greatest enemy, and my greatest motivator.

Hatred does not bloom in an instant; it takes root in small wounds, in unspoken grievances, in the quiet injustices that go unnoticed by the world. My feelings toward the Pandavas were not born out of mere envy or arrogance.

They were shaped over years, through moments that left scars, through the constant reminder that, no matter what I did, they would always be seen as superior, as more deserving.

I still remember the day they arrived in Hastinapura, five brothers standing beside their mother, Kunti. They had returned from the wilderness, from obscurity, and yet, the court received them as if they were kings reborn.

There was a shift in the air, an unspoken acknowledgment that the sons of Pandu had returned to claim what was once his.

The whispers in the halls, the stolen glances of admiration, the nods of approval from the elders—Hastinapura embraced them as if it had been waiting for them.

And in that embrace, my brothers and I found ourselves slowly being pushed aside.

Among them, it was Bhima who made his presence known the most.

He was strong, undeniably so, but he carried that strength with an unchecked arrogance. He did not see us as equals; he saw us as obstacles.

He would challenge us in games, in feats of strength, and when he won—as he often did—he laughed without restraint, as if our loss was not just expected, but inevitable.

I still recall the day he threw me into the river with ease, the water closing over my head as I struggled against the current.

He stood on the bank, laughing, unbothered by the fear that gripped me at that moment. And when my brothers suffered the same fate, it did not feel like harmless play.

It felt like a reminder—of where he believed we stood in comparison to him.

Even in the training grounds, there was always an invisible line drawn between us. Arjuna, the golden disciple, was hailed as a prodigy, the finest archer of our generation. Dronacharya, our revered teacher, showered him with praise, with knowledge, with lessons that felt deeper and more personal than what the rest of us received.

It wasn't that I did not respect Arjuna's skill—I did. But there was always the lingering question: Were we given the same opportunities? Were we ever truly being measured on equal ground?

The favoritism extended beyond the training grounds. Bhishma, our grandsire, the pillar of Hastinapura, spoke of Yudhishtira's wisdom, of Arjuna's prowess, of Bhima's strength. And us, the sons of Dhritarashtra?

We were acknowledged, but never with the same reverence. It was a subtle thing, a shift in tone, a difference in the way their names were spoken compared to ours.

Perhaps the elders did not mean to divide us in such a way, but as children, we felt it. And feelings, once rooted, grow into convictions.

Even in the smallest of matters, the Pandavas dominated. Bhima would consume more than his share of food during feasts, never pausing to consider that my brothers, too, had to eat.

It was not malicious, perhaps not even intentional, but it was symbolic of the way things always were—what they wanted, they took. And if we protested? We were the ones accused of being petty, of being envious.

It was not just about pride. It was about the slow realization that no matter what we did, the world would always look at them as the rightful heirs of Hastinapura.

My father, our king, saw this too, but he was bound by his own insecurities, by his blindness—not just of sight, but of fate itself. He wished to see us stand as equals, but he knew, as I did, that the tide was shifting away from us.

I did not wake up one morning and decide to despise the Pandavas. It was a path paved by years of being cast in their shadow, by moments that made it clear that to the world, they were the heroes of this tale, and we—my brothers and I—were merely the obstacles in their path.

I could not accept that. I would not accept that.

And so, what the world saw as rivalry, I saw as a fight for fairness. A fight to prove that our claim, our existence, was just as valid as theirs.

They taught me that the world was not fair, that destiny favored the privileged, and that power was never given—**it had to be taken.**

I did not hate them for their virtues. I hated them for the world's refusal to see mine. I hated them for the ease with which they carried their glory while I had to fight for every scrap of recognition. But most of all, I hated them because they were everything I was not: loved, celebrated, and destined for greatness.

And so, I made a vow. I would rise above them, not because I envied them, but because I needed to prove to myself—and to the world—that I was their equal. No, their better.

If the throne of Hastinapura could not be mine by birth, I would take it by will.

If dharma favored them, then I would create my own path. And when the time came, the world would remember my name, not as a villain, but as the man who fought for what was his.

Chapter 4
✦ BEYOND BLOOD ✦

When the world turned its back on me, Karna stood by my side. They call our bond opportunistic, manipulative, a partnership born of mutual need. But they are wrong. What Karna and I shared was not a mere alliance—it was brotherhood. In a world that judged us both by our circumstances of birth, we found in each other a kindred spirit, someone who understood the weight of being an outsider.

I still remember the day I first saw him. It was during the grand martial exhibition, where the Pandavas and I displayed our skills before the court and the people of Hastinapura. Arjuna, as always, stole the show, his precision with the bow drawing gasps and applause from the audience. The elders beamed with pride, the crowd chanted his name, and once again, I was relegated to the background.

And then, like a storm, Karna appeared. Dressed plainly, with none of the royal trappings that surrounded us, he stepped forward and issued a challenge to Arjuna. The crowd, initially confused by his audacity, soon fell silent as they watched him match Arjuna's every move.

His skill was undeniable, his confidence unshakable. But it was the disdain in the elders' eyes and the murmurs of the courtiers that caught my attention.

"Who is this man?" they whispered. "How dare he challenge Arjuna?"

Their contempt for him was the same contempt they reserved for me. Not because of who I was, but because of who I was *not*. Karna was not a prince. He was not born into privilege.

To them, he was an upstart, a man who had no right to stand where he did.

When Kripacharya asked for his lineage, when the question of his birth became more important than his talent, I felt a surge of anger.

Here was a man who had proven himself worthy, yet the world refused to acknowledge him simply because of the circumstances of his birth. It was a reflection of my own struggle. At that moment, I knew we were the same.

I stepped forward and declared him king of Anga. The courtiers gasped, the elders frowned, and the Pandavas glared. But Karna... Karna looked at me with an expression I will never forget.

It was gratitude, yes, but more than that, it was recognition. He saw me for what I was, just as I saw him.

At that moment, a bond was forged—a bond that no one, not even death, could break.

The world loved to whisper about the two of us. They called me manipulative, claiming I used Karna for his loyalty and skill. They called him a fool for aligning himself with a prince many deemed doomed to fail.

But those whispers meant nothing to us. We both knew the truth: our bond was forged in the fires of shared pain and defiance.

Karna's life was a constant battle against the chains of his birth. The son of a charioteer, he was denied the respect and recognition he deserved, even as he surpassed every expectation placed before him. My life, too, was a battle.

Though born a prince, I was treated as less because of my father's blindness, because of the shadow cast by the Pandavas.

Together, we stood against a world that refused to see us for what we were. We did not ask for acceptance; we demanded it. We did not wait for the world to give us our due; we took it.

Karna was more than my ally—he was my brother. There were nights when we sat together in the quiet of the palace gardens, speaking of our dreams, our frustrations, and our plans.

He never lied to me, never sugar-coated his words. He was the one person who could speak to me as an equal, without fear or hesitation.

When I doubted myself, it was Karna who reminded me of my worth. When I burned with anger, it was Karna who tempered my rage with reason.

And when the world seemed determined to crush me, it was Karna who stood beside me, unwavering in his loyalty.

The world never understood Karna. They saw him as my follower, my pawn. But Karna was no one's pawn.

He followed me not because he was weak, but because he believed in me. He saw in me the same fire that burned within him—a fire to challenge fate, to defy the gods, to carve out a place in a world that sought to deny us everything.

The Pandavas never understood our bond. They saw Karna as their enemy, a man who stood in the way of their so-called destiny. They hated him because he was a reminder that their privilege was not earned but given. Arjuna, in particular, could never stand the sight of him. He knew, deep down, that Karna was his equal, perhaps even his better. And that terrified him.

Karna's loyalty to me came at a price, and I knew it. His heart bled for the Pandavas, especially for Kunti, the mother he never knew. But he chose me, again and again, because he understood the meaning of loyalty. It wasn't about blood—it was about trust, about standing by someone who believed in you when no one else did.

The day he swore his allegiance to me was the day I knew I would never be alone. But it was also the day I knew he would suffer for that choice. The world would never forgive him for standing with me, just as it would never forgive me for standing against the Pandavas.

Chapter 5
✦ RIGHTEOUS OR CONDEMNED? ✦

They say *dharma* is eternal, unshakable and the foundation upon which the universe itself rests. But if that is true, why does *dharma* bend so easily to serve the powerful? Why does it falter when it comes to the weak, the oppressed, and the forgotten?

I have stood in the court of Hastinapura and heard the great men speak of *dharma* as though it were an unassailable truth. Bhishma, with his wisdom born of centuries, speaks of duty.

Vidura, the moral compass of the Kuru house, extols the virtues of justice. Even Yudhishtira, *The Dharmaraja,* claims to embody righteousness itself.

But when I look into their eyes, I see no answers. Only hypocrisy. Their *dharma* is nothing but a shroud—a convenient excuse to justify their privilege, their power, and their domination over others.

So I ask: what is *dharma*? And more importantly, whose *dharma* is it?

They tell me it is my duty, my *dharma,* to respect my elders. But where was Bhishma's *dharma* when my father, the rightful heir, was denied the throne because of his blindness? Where was his sense of justice when my mother was humiliated for marrying a blind man?

They tell me it is my *dharma* to serve my brothers, the Pandavas. But where is their respect for me? Am I not their cousin, their equal by blood?

Yet, from the moment they entered Hastinapura, they have looked down upon me, treating me as though I were a usurper of something that was never theirs to begin with.

They tell me it is *adharma* to covet what belongs to another. But what of the Pandavas, who claimed Indraprastha—a land that was rightfully Hastinapura's? What of Krishna, who preaches morality but uses deceit and manipulation to achieve his ends?

Dharma is not a universal truth. It is a weapon wielded by those in power to maintain their hold over the world. And I refuse to bow to it.

I have immense respect for Bhishma—how could I not? He is a man of incredible strength, unwavering will, and unmatched intellect. Yet even he is a prisoner of his so-called *dharma*.

He swore an oath of loyalty to the Kuru throne, binding himself to serve whoever sits upon it. But his *dharma* stops short of justice. When the court mocked my father for his blindness, Bhishma was silent.

When the Pandavas were given Indraprastha, Bhishma defended the decision as fair. And when I questioned these injustices, he reprimanded me for challenging the divine order.

Is that what *dharma* is? A set of chains that bind even the strongest of men? If so, **I want no part of it.**

I have been accused of *adharma* my entire life. They say my ambition is selfish, my actions cruel, my goals destructive.

But I do not see it that way. My *dharma* is not bound by the rules of the powerful; it is guided by my conscience.

It was my *dharma* to stand by Karna, a man rejected by society for his birth, and elevate him to the status he deserved.

It was my *dharma* to fight for my father, my brothers, and my people, even when the world stood against me.

If that makes me a villain, so be it. I would rather be a villain with purpose than a hero who upholds a lie.

The dice game was a moment that exposed *dharma* for what it truly was—a tool of convenience for the powerful.

Yudhishtira, gambled away his kingdom, his brothers, and even his *wife*. He justified it by saying it was his duty as a Kshatriya to accept a challenge.

But was it not also his duty to protect his people, his family, and his honor? If he was the embodiment of *dharma,* why did he allow such degradation to occur?

When Draupadi was dragged into the court, and stripped of her dignity, the court elders spoke of her chastity and purity.

But where was their outrage when Karna, a man I raised to kingship, was insulted for his caste? Why is a woman's virtue sacred but a man's lineage a stain he can never wash away?

It was at that moment I realized: *dharma* is not about justice. It is about control.

I do not reject *dharma* because I lack morals or values. I reject it because it is flawed.

My *dharma* is not dictated by the scriptures or the gods. It is dictated by my conscience, by what I see as just and fair.

It was my *dharma* to stand by Karna, a man discarded by society. It was my *dharma* to fight for my father's honor, my brothers' rights, and my kingdom's integrity.

It was my *dharma* to question the very foundation of a system that devalues the many to protect the few.

If that makes me a rebel, a villain, then so be it. But let the world know this: I fought not for power, but for change. I fought not for a throne, but for an idea.

Chapter 6
⋆ROYALTY WITHOUT A RIGHT⋆

The day I crowned Karna as the King of Anga was more than a ceremonial event; it was a declaration, a rebellion against the very foundations of the society that claimed to uphold *dharma*.

I remember the moment vividly—the grand hall of Hastinapura, the elders seated in their usual stoic silence, the Pandavas watching with barely veiled disdain, and the murmurs of disbelief rippling through the court. They whispered that I had lost my mind, that I was tarnishing the sanctity of the Kuru lineage by exalting a charioteer's son. But I didn't care for their judgment.

Karna's coronation was not for them; it was for him—and for all those who had been denied respect simply because of their birth.

The incident that led to Karna's coronation still burns in my memory. The Pandavas, with their arrogance, had mocked Karna during the display of arms, questioning his right to compete in the archery contest simply because he was a *sutaputra,* the son of a charioteer.

Arjuna, in particular, was relentless in his insults, spurred on by his pride.

Watching Karna—an unparalleled warrior, a man of immeasurable talent—reduced to an object of ridicule was unbearable.

I saw the pain in Karna's eyes, though he masked it with a stoic gaze. I knew what it meant to be looked down upon, to have your worth questioned simply because of circumstances beyond your control. In Karna, I saw a reflection of my own struggles—a man rejected not for his deeds but for his place in the rigid hierarchy of *dharma*.

When I rose from my seat and declared Karna the King of Anga, the hall fell silent. It was as if I had committed a sacrilege. I could feel the weight of disapproving stares from Bhishma, Dronacharya, and even Vidura.

They believed I was breaking the natural order, disrupting the sacred balance of caste and lineage.

But I did not care. Karna had proven himself as a warrior, as a man of honor and valor. If the Kuru court could not recognize his worth, I would force them to.

The throne of Anga, a prosperous kingdom under Hastinapura's dominion, was mine to bestow, and I chose to give it to the man who deserved it—not by birth, but by his deeds.

As I placed the crown on Karna's head, a sense of profound satisfaction filled me. It was not just a coronation; it was a proclamation.

By giving Karna the throne, I was telling the world that birth did not define a man's worth, and that courage and loyalty could shatter the chains of caste and prejudice.

Karna, humbled and overwhelmed, bowed before me. But I saw him not as a subordinate, not as a subject, but as an equal.

At that moment, I felt a bond stronger than blood—a brotherhood forged in defiance of the world that sought to suppress us.

The reactions in the court were as divided as I had expected.

The Pandavas were livid. Arjuna's face was a mask of fury, his pride wounded by the elevation of the very man he had humiliated.

Bhima, ever the brute, muttered something under his breath, no doubt an insult aimed at Karna. Yudhishtira, *The dharmaraja,* wore an expression of disapproval cloaked in righteousness, as though my decision had violated some unspoken law of the universe.

The elders were no different. Bhishma, the patriarch, looked at me with disappointment, as though I had defiled the sanctity of the Kuru dynasty.

Dronacharya's silence was colder than his words would have been, and Vidura, ever the moralist, shook his head in disapproval.

But the common people—the soldiers, the attendants, the servants—whispered in awe.

For the first time, they saw a glimmer of hope, a challenge to the rigid hierarchy that kept them bound to their fates.

Karna's coronation was not just an act of friendship; it was a revolution. By making him a king, I sought to prove a point: that greatness is not determined by lineage but by deeds. Karna had stood by me when others doubted me. He had shown courage, loyalty, and unwavering support.

In return, I gave him what he had been denied all his life— recognition, dignity, and a place among the rulers of Bharata.

I knew this act would draw criticism, that it would be seen as a reckless move driven by emotion.

But I cared little for the opinions of those who had never faced the sting of rejection or the weight of prejudice.

By crowning Karna, I did more than elevate a friend—I challenged the very concept of *dharma* that the Pandavas and their allies claimed to uphold. If *dharma* meant preserving a system that devalued a man like Karna, then I would rather defy it.

Karna was more than a king; he became a symbol of my rebellion against the societal norms that sought to dictate our lives.

His coronation was my way of telling the world that I would not bow to the hypocrisy of the so-called righteous.

From that day forward, Karna and I were bound not just by friendship but by a shared cause. He swore to fight for me, not as an obligation, but out of love and gratitude.

And I, in turn, promised to stand by him against the world that sought to belittle him.

In Karna, I found a true ally—a man who understood my struggle, my vision, and my defiance. Together, we would face the storm, challenging a world that refused to change.

Let them say what they say about that day. To me, it was not just a coronation—it was justice. And for justice, *I would defy the gods themselves.*

The great hall of Panchala shimmered with wealth and arrogance. Kings and warriors adorned in silks and jewels sat in anticipation, each believing themselves worthy of Draupadi's hand. I watched them, unimpressed. A room full of men who spoke of honor but would wield it only when convenient.

I wanted Draupadi. Who wouldn't? She was no meek princess—she was fire itself. But even as desire burned within me, I knew that to win her, skill would matter more than status. The bow, the fish's eye—this was no mere contest of names or lineage. It was a test of warriors.

And among us all, I knew who stood above the rest.

Karna.

He was already a king—the King of Anga, a title I had bestowed upon him, not out of charity, but because I saw him for what he was. A warrior beyond compare, a man whose strength eclipsed even those born into royalty. The world refused to acknowledge his greatness, but I did. And I was certain that, today, the world would have no choice but to see what I had always known.

Then he stepped forward.

Karna walked with the quiet confidence of a man who did not need to prove his worth—only to remind the world of it. There was no hesitation in his stride, no uncertainty in his movements. He reached for the bow, his gaze locked on the target.

And then, before he could even lift it, she spoke.

"I shall not wed a sutaputra."

It was not a rejection. It was an execution.

The hall fell silent. I could hear my own heartbeat, pounding like war drums in my ears. I turned to Karna, expecting outrage, expecting fury, expecting him to demand the right that was his.

But he did not.

Karna only smiled.

Not a smile of amusement. Not even a smile of bitterness. It was the smile of a man who had long made peace with the cruelty of the world. A smile that said he had expected this all along.

He did not argue. He did not demand fairness. He did not even let the insult stain his dignity. He simply stepped back, offering no words of protest, no plea for justice.

And that silence—that deafening, dignified silence—was the loudest thing in the hall.

Not a single voice rose in objection. Not the kings who had once stood trembling before his arrows. Not the warriors who had seen him stand undefeated in battle. Not even Krishna, whose silence now stood louder than words.

Karna was not denied Draupadi—he was denied respect. And that was the greatest injustice of all.

Her rejection was not just about Karna. It was a reminder to every man who had ever risen above his station that no matter how high he climbed, he would always be pulled back down by the chains of his birth.

I wanted to laugh at their hypocrisy. *If Karna was unworthy, who among them was worthy?*

And as Arjuna disguised as a Brahmin picked up the bow and took his shot, I no longer cared for the outcome.

Draupadi had made her choice.

The world had made its stand.

And I would remember.

Chapter 7
✦THE GAME OF DICE✦

The dice fell again. A soft clatter, a pause, and then silence.

The entire sabha held its breath, waiting.

Each roll of those ivory cuboids dictated the course of fate, and today, fate had chosen me.

I leaned back, feeling the cool gold of my throne press against my skin. This was no mere game—it was a reckoning.

For years, the Pandavas had been the shining beacons of virtue, the chosen ones in the eyes of the court. No matter my strength, no matter my birthright, they had always been the ones favored—by the elders, by the people, and most frustratingly, by destiny itself. Even when I had been made crown prince, their presence loomed over me like a shadow, as though the throne of Hastinapura belonged to them and I was merely a temporary occupant.

But today, they sat before me stripped of everything. Their lands, their wealth, their pride—all lost, not to my sword, but to my mind.

Shakuni's fingers idly rolled the dice in his palm, his movements slow, unhurried.

He had led Yudhishtira down this path with the patience of a master strategist, always one step ahead, always knowing exactly when to push. I had seen it before—the way he played his opponents, the way he planted thoughts in their minds so subtly that they believed the ideas were their own.

And now, Yudhishtira sat before me, his hands trembling, his forehead glistening with sweat.

His entire kingdom had crumbled in a handful of moves, and yet, he still clung to the dice as if they held the key to his redemption.

Shakuni tilted his head, observing him with something that almost looked like amusement. Then, in that same quiet, knowing voice, he spoke.

"A possession of great value still remains, my dear nephew."

I turned slightly, watching my uncle from the corner of my eye. He did not elaborate. He did not need to. The suggestion hung in the air, unspoken yet deafening.

I said nothing. I had no need to speak; Shakuni had already planted the seed.

And then Yudhishtira said it.

"I stake Draupadi."

As Yudhishtira uttered Draupadi's name, staking her as if she were nothing more than a possession in this wretched game, I leaned back and exhaled slowly. The moment was familiar—the sting of humiliation, the echo of laughter, the searing heat of disgrace. I had felt it once before, **in the cursed halls of Indraprastha.**

That day remained sharp in my memory, not because I had fallen, but because of how they had laughed.

The Mayasabha, a palace beyond the imagination of any mortal, stood as a symbol of the Pandavas' rising fortune. Maya, the Asura architect, had adorned it with illusory wonders—crystal floors that seemed like flowing water, open spaces that were in truth walls, and pools of water so still they appeared solid. **It was built to dazzle, to deceive, and it succeeded.**

As I walked through those deceptive halls, I was caught unaware.
One step forward, and the ground beneath me was no ground at all.
My foot plunged into a hidden pool, and before I could regain my
balance, I fell—soaking wet, humiliated, and seething.

Laughter rang through the hall. Bhima. Arjuna. Nakula. Sahadeva.

And then, **Draupadi.**

She, seated in splendor, turned to her maids and spoke words that
pierced deeper than any weapon, **"The blind king's son is blind
himself."**

The weight of her words crashed over me. It was not just an insult.
It was a taunt that cut through my very bloodline, a mockery of my
father, my family and my very existence.

I had risen to my feet, my fists clenched, my pride wounded beyond
measure. No one—not even the elders present—had rebuked her.
None had said it was unworthy of a queen to speak so.

And so, that day, I had sworn—I would never forget this moment.

Now, as I sat in the royal hall of Hastinapura, watching Yudhishtira
wager away his own wife, I almost laughed. How easy it was to
speak of dharma when seated on a throne. How fragile their
righteousness was when tested.

The echoes of Indraprastha still rang in my ears. **And today, the
debt was being paid.**

The moment the words left Yudhishtira's lips, a chill settled over
the sabha. The weight of what had been done pressed against the
walls and against the silent, unmoving figures of the elders.

Even the most seasoned warriors, those who had seen blood spill
on the battlefield, seemed unprepared for this.

Yet no one spoke against it.

A guard was sent to summon her. He returned, his expression uneasy. "Draupadi asks—did Yudhishtira lose himself before he lost her? If he no longer owns himself, how can he wager another?"

She was clever. She had always been clever. But words could not undo the roll of the dice.

Shakuni chuckled. "A fine argument, but she forgets the rules of the game. A wager is a wager."

And then Dhushasana moved.

With a rough grip, he seized Draupadi and dragged her into the sabha.

I watched as she struggled, her dark tresses unraveling, her saree trailing behind her like a banner of defiance. She was not a woman easily subdued.

She had stood against kings, against warriors, against fate itself. But here, at this moment, she was powerless.

All eyes were on her now. The hall that had once been filled with murmurs and whispers had fallen into complete silence.

Draupadi turned to the elders, her voice sharp. "Does no one here have the courage to stop this? Bhishma? Dronacharya? Kripacharya?"

Bhishma's lips parted, but he hesitated. The great grandsire of the Kuru dynasty, the upholder of dharma, sat silent.

Dronacharya did not lift his gaze.

Even Vidura, the lone voice of reason, seemed to struggle for words. He spoke of dharma, of justice, but his words were lost in a court that had already made its decision.

And then Karna's voice cut through the silence.

"Her husbands wagered her, and she has been lost fairly."

He did not look at her, only at the Pandavas. There was something deeper in his words—a wound unhealed, an insult remembered.

But Draupadi was undeterred.

She turned to Bhima, to Arjuna, to Yudhishtira. She did not beg, she did not plead—she demanded. And yet, none of them met her gaze.

Dhushasana sneered. "Let us see if her dignity still clings to her when nothing else does!"

And then he yanked at her saree.

The court gasped. Bhima surged forward, but he was restrained. The elders sat frozen, unwilling or unable to act.

And then Draupadi did something none of us expected.

She called upon Krishna.

Her voice rang through the sabha, clear and desperate.

"Govinda!"

The air shifted. A presence, unseen but undeniable, filled the hall.

And then—the impossible happened.

The more Dhushasana pulled, the more fabric appeared. An endless cascade of cloth, protecting her, shielding her. He tugged harder, his breath turning ragged, but no matter how much he pulled, Draupadi remained clothed.

Panic flickered in Dhushasana's eyes. He stumbled backward, his hands empty, his strength utterly useless.

And in that moment, I understood.

It was not Yudhishtira's dharma that had saved her.

Not Bhima's strength.

Not Arjuna's arrows.

It was Krishna.

The hall was silent. Shakuni's fingers had stilled over his dice. Karna said nothing. Even my own breath felt shallow.

Then, my father intervened.

Fear—for his throne, for his sons, **for the wrath of the woman standing before him**—clouded his gaze. His voice trembled as he granted Draupadi two boons.

For her first boon, she asked for Yudhishtira's freedom, and for the second, she requested the release of the other four.

He granted it.

She could have asked for more—her kingdom restored, vengeance served. But she chose dignity.

The Pandavas were leaving.

They were battered but not broken. Humiliated but not destroyed.

That could not be allowed.

I clenched my fists as I watched them step away from the sabha, Draupadi's fierce gaze burning into me like a searing flame.

Something had shifted in the air after what had happened. My father had faltered. He had undone all that we had won, gifting Draupadi boons that let the Pandavas walk away with their freedom.

It was slipping from my grasp.

I turned to Shakuni, my breath uneven. "Is this how it ends? We let them leave with their dignity? With their heads held high?"

Shakuni did not answer immediately. He was watching, thinking, calculating. His fingers traced absent patterns on the dice in his hands, the faintest smirk playing at his lips. To anyone else, he looked relaxed, unconcerned—but I knew better.

This was the moment he thrived in.

Slowly, he spoke, his voice a low murmur, meant for me alone. "Let them go? No, my dear child. We will not let them go. We will bring them back… and this time, they will lose everything."

I frowned. "How? My father has already granted them freedom."

He turned to me fully now, his eyes glinting like the very dice he wielded. "They were freed from servitude, but they were not freed from their own weakness."

He chuckled, rolling the dice between his fingers. "And what is a gambler's greatest weakness, Duryodhana?"

The answer was obvious.

The illusion of redemption.

I watched in silence as Shakuni approached Yudhishtira, his movements unhurried, his demeanor almost casual. He did not strike like a sword. He moved like a serpent—slow, silent, deadly.

The Pandavas had barely stepped out of the hall when his voice
rang out, smooth as flowing oil.

"A king does not leave a battlefield without reclaiming his honor,
does he?"

Yudhishtira stopped in his tracks. He did not turn immediately, but
I saw the way his shoulders stiffened.

"What do you mean, Mamashri?" His voice was wary.

Shakuni took a step forward, his expression unreadable. "You
played against me with your wealth and lost. That was your first
mistake." He tilted his head slightly, his tone taking on the
practiced ease of an elder offering wisdom. "But tell me, King of
Indraprastha—if wealth is lost, does that mean the game itself is
lost?"

I felt the shift in the air.

Yudhishtira hesitated. That was all Shakuni needed.

"You have lost gold, Yudhishtira. You have lost jewels and land. But
those things can be regained. Fortune is fickle, after all." His fingers
traced his dice idly. "Shouldn't a warrior seek a challenge worthy of
his name? What if this time, you wager not riches, but something
greater?"

I watched as Yudhishtira's grip tightened around the hem of his
garment. Shakuni was not just speaking to his ears—he was
speaking to his flaws.

His pride. His belief in destiny. His unshaken faith in dharma.

And just like that, the seed was planted.

Shakuni did not demand. He did not beg. He merely suggested.
And Yudhishtira, bound by the chains of his own righteousness,
walked into the trap willingly.

Shakuni turned back to me once Yudhishtira was gone, his smirk now fully formed.

"The second game has begun, my child."

I exhaled, my hands relaxing. "What will we wager this time?"

He rolled the dice between his fingers, eyes glinting. "Not wealth. Not people."

I frowned. "Then what?"

He leaned in slightly, his voice dropping lower. "Their very presence in this kingdom."

I stilled.

"Twelve years in exile," he continued, his tone laced with amusement, **"followed by a thirteenth year in disguise. If they are discovered in that final year, they repeat the exile."**

It was perfect.

A battle without swords, a war without bloodshed—yet the destruction would be absolute.

This was not just about taking Indraprastha. This was about erasing the Pandavas from the very fabric of power.

If they went into exile, they would lose more than just their kingdom. They would lose their connections, their alliances, their presence in the world of kings. They would become forgotten warriors, shadows of their former selves.

And if they failed in their thirteenth year?

They would vanish forever.

I let out a slow breath, meeting Shakuni's gaze. "You are certain he will play again?"

Shakuni merely laughed. "Yudhishtira is a man of dharma, but dharma has always been his greatest flaw. He will believe he can turn fate with his righteousness.

He will believe this time, the dice will favor him." He tossed one die into the air and caught it effortlessly. **"And that belief will be his downfall."**

The Pandavas returned. Yudhishtira, bound by his own sense of honor, had agreed.

The dice were rolled once more.

And once more, Yudhishtira lost.

I watched as their faces fell, as the weight of their fate settled upon them. There were no cries of outrage this time, no demands for justice.

Only silence.

A silence that stretched as my uncle turned to me, his voice brimming with satisfaction.

"It is done, my dear son."

Chapter 8
✦ CHAINS OF REMORSE ✦

From the outside, I was triumphant. The Pandavas, those champions of virtue and might, sat defeated in my court. Their queen, Draupadi, the woman who had dared to laugh at me, was humiliated before the assembly. I had achieved what I wanted—stripped them of their pride and reduced them to nothing. Yet, deep within me, something else stirred—an unease, a shadow of doubt that crept into my heart the moment Draupadi's humiliation turned into a divine spectacle.

When I ordered Draupadi to be disrobed, it was not a simple command. It was the culmination of my anger, my resentment, and my need to avenge every humiliation I had ever endured.

At that moment, I was a king asserting his authority, a man demanding retribution.

But when her garments became endless, my sense of control wavered.

I watched in stunned silence as Krishna—though invisible—made his presence known.

The court, which had seemed firmly in my grasp, now murmured with discontent.

Draupadi's defiance, supported by divine intervention, turned what should have been my ultimate victory into an uncomfortable, unresolved confrontation.

It was then that the first seed of guilt took root. Had I gone too far? Was my humiliation of Draupadi not just an act of revenge but a violation of something sacred?

I quickly pushed the thought aside, masking my discomfort with a veneer of anger and arrogance.

Regret is not a feeling I thought I could allow myself. As a prince of Hastinapura, I was raised to believe in my absolute right, to suppress weakness, and to never falter in pursuit of my goals. And yet, after the game of dice—after Draupadi's humiliation—I found myself grappling with a heaviness I could neither ignore nor fully understand.

The moment Draupadi was dragged into the court, I had expected satisfaction, even joy.

But what followed was far from the triumph I had imagined.

Her dignity, her fiery defiance, and her unwavering faith in Krishna turned the tide of emotions in that sabha. She stood there, wounded yet unbroken, and something in her gaze pierced through me.

At first, I convinced myself that her humiliation was justice for her laughter in the Maya Sabha, for the arrogance she wore like a crown. But the truth was more complicated.

As the court fell into an uneasy silence, as even Bhishma and Dronacharya refused to meet my eyes, I realized I had overstepped. This wasn't victory—it was something else entirely.

The weight of what I had done settled slowly, creeping into my thoughts like an unwelcome guest. Yes, I had taken Indraprastha.

Yes, the Pandavas were defeated. But at what cost? The court that had once been my playground now felt like a battlefield littered with broken ideals.

Draupadi's voice haunted me in the days that followed. Her words rang in my mind: *"Who gave you the right to stake me?"* She wasn't speaking to me directly, but I felt the question as though it had been hurled at my chest. Yudhishtira's wager was the answer, but it was a hollow justification. Somewhere deep inside, I knew that I had been complicit in something far greater than a game.

For all her vulnerability at that moment, she was not broken. Her strength, her unyielding spirit, made my victory feel small, petty.

How could I boast of defeating the Pandavas when *their queen had stood taller than me in my own court?*

The nights after the game were the hardest. Alone in my chambers, I found myself reliving the scene over and over again. I saw Draupadi being dragged into the hall, her cries for justice echoing in my ears. I remembered the looks on the faces of the elders— Vidura's disapproval, Bhishma's silence, Dronacharya's reluctance. Even Karna's loyalty, which I had always cherished, felt tainted.

In the stillness of the night, I couldn't hide from myself. The satisfaction I had expected was absent.

Instead, there was an ache, a gnawing sense of unease that I couldn't name. For the first time, I questioned not just my actions but my very motives.

Had I gone too far in my hatred for the Pandavas? Had I allowed my anger and resentment to cloud my judgment?

The sabha, which had always felt like a place of power for me, now felt hostile. Even those who remained silent during the game seemed to judge me afterward. Vidura, especially, made his disdain clear.

His words—spoken with the calm authority of a man who knew dharma—cut deeper than I cared to admit.

"Victory that dishonors dharma is no victory at all," he had said, his eyes boring into mine.

I had laughed at him then, dismissing his warnings as the ramblings of an old man. But later, when I was alone, his words echoed in my mind.

In the days that followed, I began to see the game of dice differently. What had once felt like a masterstroke of strategy now seemed like a desperate grasp for control. Yes, I had humiliated the Pandavas and claimed their kingdom.

But instead of uniting Hastinapura under my rule, I had sown seeds of discord.

The elders of the court, the people of the kingdom, even my own brothers—they all saw what I had done, and their judgment was not as silent as I had hoped.

I began to wonder if this was truly the path to power. Was my rule to be built on the humiliation of others?

Was this the legacy I wanted to leave behind—a kingdom stained by the tears of a queen and the shame of a game played without honor?

Draupadi herself became a symbol of my failure. Her fiery gaze haunted me, her voice questioning not just my actions but my very sense of justice.

I tried to bury my guilt beneath layers of anger, telling myself that she deserved what she got, that the Pandavas were the true villains.

But no matter how much I tried, I couldn't silence the voice within me that whispered otherwise. Draupadi's strength, her unwavering faith, and her ability to stand tall even in the face of humiliation made me feel small.

She had lost everything, and yet *she had won the respect of the court*—a respect I could only dream of commanding.

Despite my growing regret, I could not show it. To admit fault would be to admit weakness, and weakness was something I could not afford.

So I doubled down on my arrogance, pretending that the game of dice had been a complete victory. I surrounded myself with flatterers who assured me that I had done the right thing, that the Pandavas and Draupadi deserved their fate.

But their words rang hollow. I knew the truth, even if I refused to say it out loud. My actions had crossed a line, and no amount of justification could erase the stain they had left on my soul.

Chapter 9
✦ SHAKUNI'S GAMBIT ✦

From the very beginning, the game of dice was Shakuni's theater, and I, Duryodhana, was both his patron and his protégé. My uncle, the wily and unyielding Shakuni, was not merely a participant—he was the architect, the mastermind who transformed my burning grievances into a grand strategy of humiliation and conquest.

As I look back, it is impossible to separate my desires from Shakuni's machinations. Was he merely my ally, or was I a pawn in his game? At the time, these questions didn't matter. All that mattered was the outcome, and Shakuni promised me victory.

When the seeds of the game were first sown, it was Shakuni who watered them. I had shared my frustrations with him countless times—the Pandavas' growing strength, their prosperity in Indraprastha, and, most of all, the way they overshadowed my every achievement. My hatred burned like a raging fire, but Shakuni provided the wind to spread it.

"You cannot defeat them in war—not yet," he had told me, his voice calm, calculated.

"But in the sabha, in the game of dice, strength counts for nothing. It is cunning that wins the day."

He had a way of speaking that made everything seem inevitable, as though his plans were not just strategies but prophecies. And I, blinded by my ambition, accepted his words as truth.

Shakuni's mastery of the dice was both an art and a weapon. He played with an ease that belied the cunning behind each roll.

The loaded dice in his hands were not just tools—they were extensions of his will, a manifestation of his ability to manipulate outcomes.

He assured me that his skill would ensure our victory. "They will not suspect anything," he said, a sly smile curving his lips.

"The Pandavas are men of honor; they do not see the world as we do. They will enter the game thinking it is a test of chance, but we will make it a test of their pride—and they will fail."

It was Shakuni who recognized Yudhishtira's vulnerability—the righteous king's fatal flaw. Yudhishtira's adherence to dharma, his belief in fair play, and his unwavering faith in the sanctity of a wager were Shakuni's greatest tools.

"He cannot resist," Shakuni had whispered to me before the game began.

"Challenge his pride, appeal to his sense of honor, and he will follow wherever we lead him."

I marveled at how effortlessly Shakuni played his role.

He goaded Yudhishtira with subtle barbs, casting doubt on his courage and inviting him into the game as though it were a test of kingship. His words were like honeyed poison, sweet but deadly.

As the game progressed, it was Shakuni who guided its rhythm, ensuring that each roll of the dice tightened the noose around the Pandavas. Under his direction, the stakes escalated from gold and jewels to kingdoms and allies.

I watched as Yudhishtira, caught in the web Shakuni had spun, wagered everything he possessed in the name of honor.

When the time came to stake Draupadi, it was Shakuni who planted the idea in my mind. He saw the hesitation in me, the lingering doubt about whether such an act was too extreme.

But Shakuni, ever the master manipulator, dispelled my doubts with a simple truth:

"The greatest humiliation comes not from loss but from dishonor. Strike at their pride, and they will never recover."

His words ignited something within me. My anger, my resentment, my thirst for vengeance—all of it crystallized into a singular desire: to see Draupadi, the queen who had mocked me, brought low before the court.

Even as Draupadi was dragged into the sabha, Shakuni remained unflinching.

While others shifted uncomfortably in their seats, he leaned back, his face calm, almost amused. It was as though he were watching a play unfold, one whose ending he had already written.

But I could see the flicker of satisfaction in his eyes when Draupadi questioned her wager. He had anticipated every twist, every protest, and he responded with arguments so coldly logical that even the elders in the court struggled to counter him.

Yet, as I watched the scene unfold, I began to sense that Shakuni's satisfaction was not just for my sake.

There was something personal in his amusement, a deeper joy that went beyond my victory over the Pandavas.

Perhaps he saw Draupadi's humiliation as a strike against the Kuru dynasty itself, a dynasty he had long despised for what it had done to *his family and his kingdom.*

In the days after the game, I began to wonder about Shakuni's true motives. He had been my greatest ally, my unwavering supporter, but there were moments when I felt like a piece on his chessboard.

Was his loyalty to me genuine, or was I merely a means to his end? I knew of his hatred for the Kurus, his desire to see them brought low.

By helping me defeat the Pandavas, was he not also tearing apart the fabric of our dynasty?

At the time, I dismissed these thoughts. Shakuni had given me what I wanted—a chance to defeat the Pandavas, to claim Hastinapura as my own.

But in the quiet moments, when the weight of what we had done pressed down on me, I couldn't shake the feeling that Shakuni's game was far more intricate than I had realized.

Shakuni's role in the game of dice was undeniable. He was my strategist, my ally, and my mentor. Yet, as the consequences of the game began to unfold, I realized that his guidance came with a cost.

While I bore the brunt of the court's judgment, Shakuni remained untouched, an observer in the shadows. It was my name, not his, that was whispered with disdain.

It was my ambition that was blamed for Draupadi's humiliation, my actions that were condemned as adharmic.

In the end, I began to see Shakuni for what he truly was: a man who wielded his cunning like a blade, cutting down friend and foe alike in pursuit of his own mysterious goals.

From the moment I understood the weight of power and legacy, Krishna loomed as an unstoppable force—a divine strategist who always seemed to turn the odds in the Pandavas' favor.

For every move I made, Krishna countered with precision and foresight, leaving me to question how I could ever match his influence.

But in my uncle Shakuni, I found my answer—a mortal equal to Krishna, a man whose cunning and brilliance could bend destiny to my will.

While Krishna relied on divine authority and dharma, Shakuni was grounded in the harsh realities of life.

He was my guide, my ally, and my weapon against Krishna's righteousness.

Where Krishna's strategies were cloaked in sanctity, Shakuni wielded his cunning openly, unashamed of the deception and manipulation it required.

If Krishna was the shepherd of dharma, then Shakuni was its disruptor, and in him, I placed my trust, in even the scales of fate.

Mama had made me a promise. Not just a promise of a throne or power, but of vengeance—his own. And he fulfilled it extraordinarily.

For years, I believed he fought for me, that every move he made was to see me rule over Hastinapura. But now, as I look back, I see that his game was far greater, his vision far colder. He was never just my ally. *He was the executioner of the Kuru dynasty.*

When he first whispered into my ears, telling me how I had been wronged, how my birthright was denied, I believed he saw what I saw—an injustice. But he saw something different. He saw the *Kurus*—all of them, Pandavas and my own brothers alike—as those responsible for his father's suffering. For his family's doom.

And so he played the long game.

He orchestrated the downfall of Hastinapura with precision, with patience, with an unyielding hatred that even I had failed to grasp.

The game of dice had been his battlefield long before Kurukshetra. He had destroyed Yudhishthira's honor, broken Draupadi's spirit, shattered the Pandavas' pride—and I, in my arrogance, had believed it was for me. I had thought he waged this war to see me triumph.

But Shakuni never waged a war for me.

He waged a war for himself.

When Dushasana fell, bleeding his last into the soil, *he did not grieve.*
When my ninety-nine brothers were slain, *he did not weep.*
When my father sat frozen, helpless in his blindness, mourning his lost sons, *he did not comfort him.*

Because he had already won.

The Kurus were destroyed. Pandavas or Kauravas, it did not matter to him. **We were all Kuru**. And his vengeance was complete.

Had I been a mere instrument of his revenge? A pawn, blinded by my own ambitions, while he orchestrated the fall of an empire?

No. **I refuse to believe that.**

Yet the doubt lingers, settling into my bones like a poison. The weight of his victory hangs over me like a shadow, whispering a truth I do not want to accept.

Mama kept his promise. He had ensured that the House of Kuru—**all of it**—would crumble.

Even if it meant watching me fall with it.

Chapter 10
✦ TWO MINDS, ONE WAR ✦

Krishna was a god among men, and his words carried the weight of celestial wisdom. Shakuni, by contrast, was all too human—a man who had suffered, bled, and burned in the fires of loss. He did not speak of dharma or cosmic order; he spoke of survival, of power, and of revenge.

"Your kingdom," he once told me, "does not belong to the righteous. It belongs to the strong. Krishna might preach dharma, but it is men like us—those who take, those who refuse to be denied—who shape the world."

I remember the clarity of his words. At that moment, I understood the stark truth: to rise above Krishna's divine machinations, I needed a weapon that wasn't bound by the illusions of morality. Shakuni became that weapon. He taught me to see the world not as it should be, but as it is—a battlefield where only the ruthless survive.

The sabha during the game of dice was where Shakuni's genius shone brightest. While Krishna chose the battlefield to enact his will, Shakuni turned the Kuru court into his stage.

Each roll of his dice was a calculated step toward dismantling the Pandavas, and I, his protégé, relished every moment.

Shakuni saw Yudhishtira's weakness long before I did. "He clings to dharma like a drowning man to driftwood," he told me. "All we must do is show him a game where he believes his honor is at stake, and he will drown himself."

True to his word, Shakuni lured Yudhishtira into the game with masterful precision. Krishna's influence over the Pandavas was no match for Shakuni's ability to exploit human frailty. While Krishna guided them with divine sermons and visions of destiny, Shakuni understood their flaws intimately—Yudhishtira's pride, Arjuna's hesitance, Draupadi's fire. He knew how to turn these virtues into vulnerabilities.

Where Krishna acted as an incarnation of Vishnu, bearing the weight of cosmic order, Shakuni was a man forged by the chaos of his own life. His hatred for the Kurus—born from the tragedy of Gandhara, where his family had been reduced to pawns in a dynastic game—fueled his every action.

Some might say that Krishna's divinity gave him an advantage, but I saw things differently.

Shakuni's humanity made him unpredictable, adaptable. Krishna's morality was rigid, bound by the constraints of dharma.

Shakuni, unshackled by such ideals, operated in a realm where the ends justified the means. He didn't preach; he acted.

To me, Krishna's divinity often felt distant, even suffocating. His righteousness demanded sacrifices that I could never make.

Shakuni's cunning, however, was tangible and empowering. He didn't demand faith—he demanded results.

As I watched Krishna maneuver the Pandavas, I saw a man who could twist dharma to suit his needs.

His ability to justify even the most questionable actions—be it advising Arjuna to kill Karna when he was unarmed or encouraging Bhima to strike me in the thigh—proved that even dharma could be a weapon in the right hands.

Shakuni, on the other hand, never pretended to be righteous. He wielded pragmatism like a blade, cutting through the illusions of morality that Krishna so often used to shroud his actions. "Dharma is a tool of the powerful," Shakuni once said.

"Do not let it enslave you. Use it when it serves you, discard it when it doesn't."

This philosophy became my creed. While Krishna's Pandavas fought for a vision of justice that was always just out of reach, Shakuni and I fought for something far more real: *victory, at any cost.*

Shakuni was not merely my uncle; he was my strategist, my confidant, and, at times, my conscience. His counsel was sharp, often brutal, but it never faltered. When I doubted myself, when the weight of Krishna's influence seemed insurmountable, it was Shakuni who reminded me of my purpose.

"Krishna might win hearts," he told me, "but we win minds. And in the end, it is the mind that rules the world."

I believed him. Every triumph I achieved—every humiliation of the Pandavas, every inch of power I wrested from their grasp—was a testament to Shakuni's brilliance.

In many ways, Shakuni was Krishna's mirror. Both men shaped destiny, but they did so in opposite ways. Krishna sought to uphold a divine order, while Shakuni sought to dismantle it. Krishna inspired with hope; Shakuni commanded with logic.

To me, they were two sides of the same coin. Krishna's actions, though wrapped in dharma, were just as calculated as Shakuni's. The difference lay in their presentation. Krishna cloaked his strategies in righteousness, while Shakuni wielded his cunning without apology.

Though Krishna ultimately prevailed in the grand scheme, I cannot help but admire the audacity of Shakuni's defiance. He stood against a divine force, not with celestial powers but with his mortal intellect. Every move Krishna made was countered by Shakuni with equal precision, and for a time, it seemed as though the gods themselves could be challenged by the will of a single man.

To me, Shakuni was more than just an ally—he was my weapon against Krishna's divine interference.

He proved that even the grandest designs of gods could be unraveled by mortal cunning.

In Shakuni, I saw the power of humanity: its ability to defy, to adapt, to conquer.

While Krishna remains immortalized as the preserver of dharma, Shakuni's legacy lies in his audacity to challenge it.

Together, they shaped the Mahabharata as a battle not just of kingdoms, but of ideologies—a clash between divinity and humanity, between dharma and pragmatism. And as I stood by Shakuni's side, I realized that his brilliance was my greatest weapon, even against the might of the gods.

Chapter 11
✦WHERE RIVALRY MEETS REVERENCE✦

Krishna. His name alone carried weight, power, and reverence in the world of Aryavarta. To many, he was Vasudeva, the divine strategist, the upholder of dharma, and the beloved god. To me, however, Krishna was more than just a rival or an adversary. He was a figure I could not ignore, a man who, despite my resentment, commanded my respect.

In the stillness of my own thoughts, I often found myself torn when it came to Krishna. How could I not admire him? He was a man whose mere presence tilted the balance of power. Even when I hated him, even when I sought to undermine him, I could not deny his brilliance.

From the moment Krishna entered the political stage, he became the center of every conversation. He wasn't just a king of Dwaraka; he was the kingmaker of Aryavarta.

People listened when he spoke, and even the most obstinate warriors and rulers bent to his will.

I envied this power, but I also admired it. Krishna had the rare ability to transform words into weapons, to sway the hearts of even his enemies.

When he convinced the Yadavas to leave Mathura and build a fortress city in Dwaraka, I marveled at his foresight. He turned what could have been a defeat into an unparalleled triumph.

Though I hated how Krishna often championed the Pandavas, I could not help but recognize his strategic genius. He never fought with a sword or mace, yet he won wars before they even began.

If Shakuni was my guiding hand in the sabha, Krishna was the Pandavas' guiding force on the battlefield of life.

Krishna wasn't just intelligent—he was magnetic. He had a charm that I, despite all my wealth and power, could never replicate.

I was born into the Kuru dynasty, the mightiest lineage of Aryavarta. Yet, Krishna, a cowherd by birth, stood shoulder to shoulder with the greatest of kings.

There was something in his presence that disarmed people. When Krishna entered a room, he filled it with an aura of calm and command. Even I, who considered him my adversary, could feel it.

I remember the time he came to Hastinapura as an emissary of the Pandavas, seeking peace before the Kurukshetra war.

He walked into the Kuru court unarmed, without fear, his head held high. Every word he spoke was measured, every gesture deliberate. He wasn't just pleading the Pandavas' case—he was commanding us to reconsider. For a brief moment, I almost wanted to listen. That was Krishna's power: the ability to make even his enemies question their convictions.

What struck me most about Krishna was his mastery of dharma. While others, including myself, struggled with its complexities, Krishna wielded it like a sword.

He could justify anything—war, peace, deceit—under the banner of dharma.

There were moments when I questioned whether Krishna truly upheld dharma or merely manipulated it.

He advised Arjuna to kill Karna when he was unarmed, and he orchestrated the killing of Bhishma and Dronacharya through cunning rather than strength. Was this dharma? To me, it felt like a calculated strategy. Yet, the world revered him for it.

I often wondered if this was Krishna's true genius: his ability to bend dharma without breaking it. He made the world believe that even his most questionable actions were righteous. I envied that skill, for I had no such luxury. When I acted, I was branded as arrogant, impulsive, or cruel. But Krishna? Krishna turned every decision into a divine act.

What pained me most about Krishna was the constant comparison. In the eyes of the world, Krishna was the ideal leader—wise, selfless, and invincible. And I? I was the ambitious prince, consumed by envy and greed.

The people adored Krishna. They sang songs of his exploits, his childhood adventures, his victories, and his wisdom.

No one sang songs for me. No one celebrated my triumphs or my vision for Hastinapura.

If Krishna had been born in my place, would the world have loved him as they loved me? Or was it Krishna's humility, his ability to remain unattached to power, that made him so revered?

My feelings toward Krishna were complex—a mix of admiration, envy, and resentment. I admired his brilliance, his ability to inspire loyalty and respect. But I hated how easily he overshadowed me, how he became the benchmark against which I was measured.

There were times when I wished I could sit with Krishna, not as a rival but as an equal. I wanted to understand how his mind worked, how he saw the world. Did he ever doubt himself? Did he ever struggle with the weight of his choices?

But such a conversation was impossible. Krishna and I were destined to stand on opposite sides of the battlefield, each representing a different vision of the world.

Sometimes, in my darkest moments, I saw Krishna as a reflection of what I could have been.

If fate had been kinder, if the Kuru court had treated me with the respect I deserved, perhaps I too could have been a figure like Krishna.

I often asked myself: what separated us? Was it merely circumstance? Or was there something intrinsic to Krishna that I lacked? These questions haunted me, for they forced me to confront my own insecurities.

 I watched him. From the corner of my eye, from across the grand halls of Hastinapura, from the edges of battlefields where fates were decided—I watched him

His name alone carried a weight I could never escape. *The wielder of Sudarshana, the cowherd who ruled over hearts, the voice that silenced great kings, the very force that shaped destiny.*

And yet, for all my strength, for all my victories, for all the ways I carved my own path, I could never get him to look at me the way he looked at them.

The Pandavas.

To them, he was a charioteer, a counselor, a shield against ruin. **To me, he was a god who had already chosen his side.** And yet, some part of me—some pathetic, desperate part of me—wanted him to see me too. To acknowledge me. To say that I was more than the villain they had painted me to be.

I knew better than to ask for his guidance—I could never show such weakness. But did he not see? Did he not see that I, too, sought wisdom? That I, too, wanted to be told that my path was just? That I, too, longed for the voice that had shaped kings to tell me that I was not beyond redemption?

But he never did.

When he came as a messenger of peace, I knew what I had to do. I laughed in his face, mocked his words, called his diplomacy futile. What else could I do? Beg for his approval like a child?

I had spent a lifetime pretending I did not care for the gaze that never turned my way.

Yet, when he stood before me, when he spoke with that unshakable calm, when his eyes—so unreadable, so godlike—settled on me even for a moment, I felt the weight of it. For a fraction of a breath, I believed he might say something—anything—that would make me feel as if *I mattered in his world.*

But he did not.

He had already chosen.

But even as I walked away, even as I stood firm in my defiance, some part of me—some small, bitter part—ached for a different truth.

A truth where Krishna had once turned to me and said, **"Duryodhana, I see you too."**

Chapter 12
✦"A WOMAN WRONGED, A WAR FORETOLD."✦

The disrobing of Draupadi in the Kuru court is a moment that casts a shadow over my life—a moment I cannot think about without a storm of conflicting emotions. It was not a mere incident; it was a turning point that shaped the destiny of Hastinapura and the fate of the Kuru dynasty.

Even now, I cannot look back on that day without feeling the weight of guilt, regret, and shame.

It began as a game—a calculated move orchestrated by Shakuni and myself to assert dominance over the Pandavas, to expose their vulnerabilities, and to reclaim what I believed was rightfully mine.

When Yudhishtira staked Draupadi after losing himself in the game of dice, it wasn't a scenario I had envisioned. In my mind, the game was always about kingdoms and power, about pride and proving superiority. But when Draupadi's name entered the wager, the atmosphere of the court shifted.

As Draupadi was summoned to the court, I was intoxicated with the thrill of victory.

My lifelong rivalry with the Pandavas, my resentment of their favor with the elders, and my determination to prove myself as the rightful heir to the Kuru throne—all of it culminated at that moment.

But in my arrogance, I failed to see the line I was crossing.

The court erupted in chaos as Draupadi refused to come, sending back the question that still echoes in my ears: *"How could a man who has lost himself wager someone else?"* The question was valid, but I, blinded by my pride, dismissed it as insolence.

When Draupadi was dragged into the court by Dushasana, I watched with satisfaction as the Pandavas sat helplessly, their heads bowed in shame. For me, it was a moment of triumph, a public demonstration of their vulnerability. But I failed to recognize the horror unfolding before my eyes.

As Draupadi stood before us, her fiery gaze cutting through the court, I remember being struck by her defiance. She was no ordinary woman; she was a queen, proud and fearless, even in her humiliation.

Yet, at that moment, her strength became a threat to my pride.

When she questioned the legitimacy of the wager, challenging the elders and the court, my frustration grew. Her refusal to submit, her audacity to speak against me and my kin, felt like an affront I could not tolerate. My pride demanded that I put her in her place, and in my arrogance, I mistook humiliation for power.

It was then that I made the fatal gesture, slapping my thigh and mocking her to sit on it. I remember the laughter that followed— laughter that now haunts me.

It was not just my pride speaking; it was my insecurity, my need to assert dominance in a court that had always treated me as second to the Pandavas.

In the heat of the moment, I ignored the unease in the room. Vidura's protests, Bhishma's silence, and even Karna's discomfort were drowned out by my need to humiliate the Pandavas.

There was a fleeting moment when my eyes met Draupadi's. Her gaze was not just angry; it was filled with disbelief and sorrow. That moment stayed with me, even as Dushasana attempted to disrobe her. I remember looking away, unable to face what was happening. Somewhere deep within, a voice screamed that this was wrong, that this was not the victory I had sought.

But I was too consumed by my pride to act on that voice. I let the atrocity unfold, clinging to the belief that this was my rightful revenge, that I was teaching the Pandavas a lesson they would never forget.

When Draupadi called upon Krishna, and her saree became endless, the court fell silent. For the first time that day, I felt the weight of my actions. This was not a game anymore; it was an affront to dharma itself. The divine intervention was not just a miracle—it was a rebuke, a reminder of the line we had crossed.

At that moment, I saw the court for what it had become: a place of chaos, dishonor, and shame. And I saw myself for what I had allowed myself to become: a man blinded by ambition, willing to trample over the dignity of a woman to satisfy his ego.

The days that followed were heavy with the aftermath of that fateful moment. The Pandavas' silent rage, Draupadi's fiery vow, and the disapproval of the court elders—all of it weighed on me.

I began to realize that my actions had not just humiliated Draupadi; they had tainted the Kuru dynasty.

I often replayed that day in my mind, questioning every decision. Why had I allowed my pride to push me so far? Why had I not stopped Dushasana?

Why had I, a prince of Hastinapura, chosen humiliation over honor?

Regret gnawed at me, but it was too late to undo what had been done. Draupadi's curse, her vow to see my downfall, became a shadow that loomed over me. Every triumph felt hollow, every victory tainted by the memory of her humiliation.

Over time, I came to understand the true cost of that day. It wasn't just about losing the moral high ground; it was about losing a part of myself. In my desire to defeat the Pandavas, I had strayed so far from the ideals I claimed to uphold.

The disrobing of Draupadi was not just a stain on my legacy; it was a wound in my soul. It reminded me of my own fallibility, of how easily pride and ambition can lead a man astray.

Even as I prepared for the Kurukshetra war, the memory of Draupadi's humiliation haunted me.

Her fiery gaze, her voice echoing in the court, her invocation of Krishna—they were reminders of a moment when I had failed not just as a prince but as a human being.

She was no ordinary woman. She was no mere queen.

She was Draupadi. And she had just sealed our fates.

She did not need a sword or an army. Her rage was enough. She vowed then and there, with fire in her voice, that this humiliation would not go unanswered. The Pandavas, stripped of their kingdom, had lost everything that day—but we had lost something far greater.

We had made an enemy of a woman whose wrath could burn down empires.

As I met her gaze, unrelenting and filled with fury, I knew—this was no longer about a throne, a kingdom, or a game of dice. This was war, written in the language of vengeance.

And there was no turning back.

Chapter 13
✦THE MAKING OF AN ARMY✦

The journey to assemble allies for the great war of Kurukshetra was as much a test of diplomacy and resolve as it was a demonstration of my vision for a united front against the Pandavas. The Pandavas, with their virtuous facade and Krishna's cunning guidance, had always managed to capture the sympathies of kings and commoners alike. I, however, had to rely on something more human—understanding grievances, appealing to ambition, and forging bonds that would stand the test of battle.

The process began with careful calculations and deliberations. I knew that strength lay in numbers and influence, but not all allies were equal.

Some joined willingly, while others needed persuasion. Each alliance had to be crafted, each ruler approached with a plan that resonated with their aspirations and struggles.

I couldn't rely on divine blessings like the Pandavas; instead, I depended on my ability to see the world as it was, to understand the hearts of men, and to appeal to the parts of them that sought power, recognition, or revenge.

Shalya, the mighty king of Madra and maternal uncle to the Pandavas, was one such challenge. His arrival to support his nephews would have tilted the scales significantly.

Learning of his journey to their camp, I intercepted him with the finest hospitality Hastinapura could provide.

The grandeur of my welcome was not mere extravagance; it was a message—a declaration that I valued his strength, his reputation, and his worth as a ruler.

Shalya eventually pledged his allegiance, not through coercion but through a recognition of the respect and value I placed on him.

There were others who joined for their own reasons, and I knew how to nurture those reasons. The Trigartas, fierce warriors with a long-standing grudge against Arjuna, saw an opportunity in my cause to challenge the Pandava who had repeatedly humiliated them.

Bhagadatta of Pragjyotisha, a king tied by legacy to the Kuru throne, stood with me out of loyalty to his lineage. Each ally brought with them their own grievances, ambitions, and strengths, and I ensured that they saw my cause as their own.

Karna, my most trusted friend and ally, was instrumental in this effort. His voice carried the weight of conviction, and his story of rejection resonated with those who felt wronged by the world. He visited distant kingdoms, recounting not only his journey but also the injustices I had faced.

Karna was more than a warrior; he was a beacon of my vision for a world where loyalty, merit, and strength mattered more than bloodlines. With his help, I reached places my presence alone could not.

Even kings with personal enmities against the Pandavas found their way into my fold. Jayadratha, who had been insulted and defeated by them, saw this war as his chance to reclaim his honor.

The Kambojas, who valued strength above all, recognized that my forces would offer them a battlefield to prove their might.

Shakuni, my uncle and mentor, orchestrated many of these negotiations with his sharp wit and intricate strategies. Each alliance was a testament to the shared grievances and ambitions that bound us together.

The task of assembling allies was not merely transactional; it was deeply personal. Every king who stood with me was not just a name on a list; they were individuals who believed in the same vision I had—a world where the sanctimonious claims of dharma would be challenged and exposed.

Together, we represented those who had been wronged, overlooked, or underestimated by a system that favored divine intervention over human effort.

The war drums of Kurukshetra had not yet begun to thunder, but I knew the time was near. Gathering allies was not just a matter of strategy; it was a battle in itself. Every king, every commander, every warrior I sought had their own grievances, their own ambitions.

Some pledged their loyalty because they saw justice in my cause, while others did so for their own reasons. Yet, among all the alliances I forged, one stood above the rest—**The Narayani Sena.**

It was an irony even the gods must have found amusing. Krishna, the very man who stood against me, had an army feared across Bharata. Thousands of warriors, disciplined, battle-hardened, and utterly devoted to their master.

It was said that even the mightiest armies trembled at the sight of Krishna's Narayani Sena marching onto the battlefield. And I had secured them for my side.

The day I rode into Dwaraka, my mind was clear. Krishna and Arjuna were there before me, seeking the same thing—a force that could tip the scales of war. But what awaited us in Krishna's chamber was a choice unlike any other.

The wielder of the Sudarshana Chakra, the divine strategist himself, lay asleep on his grand bed when we arrived. As per custom, the one who entered first had the right to make the first request. I, being the earlier arrival, stood proudly at the head of his bed, while Arjuna, ever the humble devotee, stood at his feet.

When Krishna finally opened his eyes, he looked upon Arjuna first. My blood burned at the unfairness of it, but I held my composure. He smiled, acknowledging us both, and then spoke. "You both have come for my aid, but I shall offer you a choice."

A choice. I knew already that fate had its own twisted way of dealing cards, but I had to listen. Krishna laid out his terms—on one side was he, alone, unarmed, vowing not to lift a weapon in battle.

On the other side, his mighty Narayani Sena, ready to fight and die for whoever commanded them.

I did not hesitate.

War was not won by divine words or the wisdom of a man who refused to fight. War was won by blood, by steel, by the strength of warriors who could turn the tide with their sheer might. Krishna, standing alone, would be nothing more than a spectator. But his army—his army would march under my banner. I made my choice with confidence, my voice steady, my heart triumphant. "I choose the Narayani Sena."

Arjuna, in his ever-smug humility, folded his hands and said he would take Krishna. He spoke of devotion, of divine blessings, of how having Krishna by his side was a greater fortune than having an entire army. Foolishness, I thought. He had left me with the true advantage, and I took it without a second thought.

As I rode back from Dwaraka, my heart swelled with satisfaction. The great Yadava warriors, trained under Krishna's watchful eyes, would now fight for me.

Clad in gleaming armor, wielding swords that had known the taste of countless battles, their loyalty was unshakable, their discipline unmatched. I saw them line up, their formations precise, their resolve firm. They were ready to fight and die for my cause.

For all of Arjuna's faith in Krishna's presence, I had secured what mattered most in war—strength in numbers, warriors with unmatched prowess. I knew then, that I had made the right decision.

As I stood in the grand halls of Hastinapura, surrounded by the kings, princes, and warriors who had pledged their loyalty, I felt a surge of determination.

This was not merely an army; it was a coalition of shared purpose, a force that believed in my right to stand against the Pandavas and their god-backed claims.

The Kurukshetra war was no longer just about a throne; it was about justice—justice for those who had been cast aside, insulted, and ignored.

Looking out at the gathering of allies, I felt an overwhelming sense of purpose. This war would not only define the fate of the Kuru dynasty but also the very nature of dharma itself. I would fight not just for myself but for every voice that had been silenced, for every ruler who sought fairness in a world ruled by divine politics. I would prove that strength, ambition, and resilience were as sacred as any divine decree.

This was my war to win.

Chapter 14
✦BETWEEN DHARMA AND DEVOTION✦

Karna was more than a friend to me; he was the embodiment of loyalty, resilience, and the defiance of fate. In a world where birth determined worth and bloodlines dictated respect, Karna stood as a shining example of a man who rose above such limitations. From the moment I first met him, standing humiliated at the Pandavas' contest, I saw in him a reflection of my own struggles—a man cast aside, misunderstood, and underestimated.

It was at that moment that I realized I had found not just a companion but a kindred spirit. His fire, his hunger to prove himself, mirrored my own ambition. I extended my hand to him not out of pity but out of recognition. Karna deserved to stand alongside the greatest warriors of our time, not in their shadow. Elevating him as the king of Anga was not just a strategic move; it was a statement—a declaration that merit mattered more than privilege.

Karna's prowess on the battlefield was unparalleled. Even Arjuna, with his celestial weapons and Krishna's divine guidance, knew that facing Karna was no simple task.

Karna fought with an intensity that came from years of being denied what was rightfully his.

Every swing of his mace, every arrow he released, carried the weight of his struggle.

To my cause, Karna was not just a warrior but a symbol—a symbol that *the greatest talents often came from unexpected places*. His victories on the battlefield rallied our soldiers, his courage inspiring even the most hesitant among them. When Karna led a charge, he did so with the conviction of a man who had nothing to lose and everything to prove.

Karna's role was not limited to the battlefield; he was also my most trusted emissary. While Shakuni excelled at crafting strategies and manipulating outcomes, Karna brought a raw honesty to our mission. When I needed to build alliances, Karna's presence often tipped the scales.

He spoke not of divine blessings or destiny but of human strength and perseverance. His story resonated with kings who had faced rejection or who sought recognition. Karna understood their struggles because they were his own. He could connect with them in ways no one else could, convincing them that our cause was just.

It was Karna who reminded our allies that we were fighting not against righteousness but against hypocrisy.

The Pandavas, with their celestial weapons and Krishna's divine guidance, claimed to fight for dharma, but they were just as fallible as any of us. Karna's words cut through their pretense, exposing the Pandavas for what they were—humans who hid behind divine favor.

Karna and I shared an unspoken bond that went beyond words. We both understood what it meant to be underestimated and rejected. I never saw Karna as an outsider or as a man of low birth; to me, he was my equal, my brother in spirit.

He stood by me not for wealth or power but because he believed in me.

He saw the unfairness in how the Pandavas claimed virtue while I was vilified.

He knew that I fought not for mere ambition but for justice, for a world where people like us could rise without being shackled by the circumstances of our birth.

Karna's loyalty was unwavering, even in the face of death. When Krishna revealed his true lineage as Kunti's son, offering him a place among the Pandavas, Karna refused. He chose me, knowing full well the consequences. That choice cemented my belief in him as the most honorable man I had ever known.

Despite his strength, Karna carried a deep burden. The curse of his guru, Parashurama, and the celestial armor he surrendered weighed heavily on him.

I could see it in his eyes—a flicker of doubt, a shadow of inevitability. He never spoke of it, but I knew he was aware of the uphill battle he faced.

In the quiet moments before battle, I would catch him staring into the distance, lost in thought.

It pained me to see him bear such a heavy load, knowing that fate itself seemed determined to conspire against him.

Yet, even under such weight, he never wavered in his commitment to me or our cause.

On the battlefield of Kurukshetra, Karna was my anchor. His presence gave me strength, his victories bolstered my resolve. Even as the war progressed and the odds tilted in favor of the Pandavas, Karna stood firm.

He fought like a lion, unyielding even in the face of Krishna's cunning strategies and Arjuna's divine weapons.

When the fateful duel between Karna and Arjuna finally came, I watched with bated breath. My heart sank when Karna's chariot wheel sank into the earth, a cruel twist of fate that sealed his end.

Even then, he fought with valor, refusing to surrender to destiny. His death was not just a loss to me but a loss to the entire war.

Karna's death marked the beginning of the end for us. Yet, even in death, he remained a symbol of resilience. He proved that greatness could rise from anywhere, that loyalty and merit mattered more than divine blessings.

The battlefield of Kurukshetra raged like an unchained storm. Blood soaked the earth, war cries echoed in the air, and the sky itself seemed to darken under the weight of slaughter.

Yet amidst this chaos, one battle held the power to shift the fate of the war—the clash between **Karna and Arjuna.**

I stood still, my breath heavy, my gaze locked on the battlefield. *This was the moment.*

Arjuna—the wielder of *Gandiva*, the favorite of the gods, the warrior whose victories were sung in every corner of Bharatavarsha—now faced a force he had never truly reckoned with.

Karna.

The man who had risen from ridicule, who had endured humiliation, yet wielded the strength of Indra himself. He stood now, not just as the King of Anga, but as the warrior fate had always wronged—yet never defeated.

Their chariots blazed across the battlefield, kicking up dust as arrows rained like a relentless storm. Arjuna's chariot was not just any chariot.

It was a gift from Agni Deva himself, bearing the divine protection of Hanuman's banner fluttering above, symbolizing the strength of the mighty vanara. And at its reins stood Krishna—the supreme protector, the eternal guide.

That chariot was a fortress. Anchored by the will of divinity itself, it seemed immovable, unshakable. And yet—

Karna pulled back the string of his *Vijaya bow*. The great bow that had once belonged to Parashurama, the very weapon that even the gods feared. His arms did not waver, his gaze did not falter. At that moment, he was beyond mortal. He was a force bound by neither destiny nor doubt.

Then, he released the arrow.

The battlefield itself seemed to tremble. A divine shaft, burning like the sun itself, cut through the air with an intensity that made the heavens pause. Arjuna met it with his own, and when the two celestial arrows collided—

The impossible happened.

Arjuna's chariot, blessed by Agni, shielded by Hanuman, and guided by Krishna himself, **lurched backward—two full steps.**

A stunned silence fell upon the battlefield. Warriors on both sides—Kaurava and Pandava—froze in their places. A mere mortal had forced the gods to retreat.

For a brief moment, I turned my gaze towards Krishna. For the first time, I saw something in his expression. It was not fear, nor was it surprise. But it was acknowledgment. A silent acceptance of the power Karna wielded.

And then, before the awe could settle, **Karna's chariot reeled back—ten full steps.**

Arjuna's lips curled into a smirk. He turned to Krishna, his voice laced with pride.

"Did you see, Madhava? My arrow struck Karna with such force that his chariot moved ten steps, while mine barely moved two."

Krishna remained calm, his gaze still on Karna. And then, with quiet authority, he spoke.

"Do you know why, Partha? Because your chariot carries the weight of the divine. Hanuman's protection shields you, the boon of Agni fortifies you, and I stand at your reins. Despite all this, Karna's arrow pushed you back two steps. *Imagine, had you been without these protections, what might have happened?*"

Arjuna's smirk faded. I saw understanding settle upon his face.

Karna, that man of unrelenting will, had fought against the will of gods themselves. He was a warrior not cradled by fate, but beaten by it, yet he still stood—undaunted, unwavering.

And the moment, his chariot steadied once more, I realised the truth.

The gods had chosen their warrior, but destiny had forged its own.

The world has always whispered of Karna's so-called fate. They say he was born cursed, that the gods themselves wove his misfortune into the very fabric of destiny. But I refuse to believe that. The gods did not curse Karna. They feared him.

And what does a man do when he fears another? He does not fight him honorably. He deceives him. He robs him of what makes him great.

Indra, the king of the Devas, did not descend from his golden throne to test Karna's generosity out of admiration.

He came because he knew—if Karna stood on the battlefield with his golden armor, with his celestial earrings, *even Arjuna, his own son, would stand no chance.*

Karna had been born with the divine **Kavacha and Kundala**—his celestial armor and earrings, gifts from Surya himself. They were not merely ornaments, not mere shields. They were Karna's protection from every force in the universe. No weapon, no divine missile, no celestial strike could harm him as long as he bore them. With them, he was invincible.

And so Indra—cowardly, cunning Indra—came to him in disguise. Not as a god, not as the mighty wielder of the Vajra, but as a frail Brahmin, his hands folded in supplication.

"Give me alms, O Karna," he said, his voice laced with false humility.

Karna—who had known nothing but rejection, nothing but dishonor—stood by his vow. The world had stripped him of his birthright, his dignity, his truth, but it could never take away his generosity.

He saw not a god in disguise, not an enemy, but a man in need. And so, without hesitation, he cut away his divine armor from his own flesh.

He peeled away his celestial earrings, letting blood drip from his ears, all to honor a dharma the world never honored for him.

Indra, satisfied in his deceit, had no gratitude. Only relief. Relief that Arjuna's greatest threat had been tamed before the war had even begun.

And what did Karna receive in return?

A weapon—the Vasavi Shakti. A spear of unparalleled power, but **one he could use only once**. A mere trade, a hollow compensation for what was stolen from him.

And I? I raged.

When he stood before me, blood trickling down his chest where his armor once was, I did not see a man humbled. I saw a warrior who had been betrayed by the very heavens.

"Karna!" I thundered. "Why? Why did you not deny him? Why did you not send him away?"

He only smiled, weary yet unwavering. *"Because, my friend, a man does not choose the nature of his birth. But he does choose the nature of his actions."*

I clenched my fists, anger boiling in my veins. Was that not always Karna's tragedy? That his honor was greater than the world's? That his righteousness was repaid only with treachery?

And the gods, the celestial beings who called themselves just, stood silent. They did not punish Indra for his deception. They did not curse him for his theft.

Because it was never about justice. It was about keeping Karna from becoming what he was meant to be—the greatest warrior of our age.

Had he stood with his armor and earrings intact, even Krishna would have thought twice before stepping onto the battlefield.

But they stripped him of that power, just as they had stripped him of his birthright.

And yet, Karna did not waver. He did not curse the gods, nor did he question fate. He stood, still proud, still unbroken.

Perhaps that was the greatest revenge of all.

Deception had become the Pandavas' greatest weapon—more lethal than Arjuna's Gandiva, more cunning than Krishna's words.

They had already robbed Karna of his invincibility, stripping him of his divine kavacha and kundalas with sweet words and false praise. *But where was honor in war, when the Pandavas themselves resorted to trickery?*

And then, they turned their deceit upon **our Acharya.**

Dronacharya was a fortress in himself, a warrior none could surpass. His celestial weapons alone could have turned the tide of war in our favor. And yet, they did not face him in battle.

They did not fight.

They schemed.

Bhima, ruthless as ever, struck down an elephant named Ashwatthama—a name that belonged to our Acharya's son.

I remember that moment like a wound that never closed.

Dronacharya's chariot... it always hovered. Not by spell or sorcery — but by virtue. Such was the weight of his dharma, or perhaps the lightness of it, that even the earth refused to press against his wheels.

We'd all seen it, day after day, battle after battle — his chariot floating an inch above the ground, untouched by the dust and blood below. It was a sight that made gods pause and men revere.

But that day, when Yudhishthira — the man known for truth — uttered those words, *"Ashwatthama is dead"*... the sky itself seemed to falter. And then, as if truth had been betrayed and righteousness undone, the impossible happened — the great chariot of Drona, for the first time, **gently descended**... and touched the earth.

It didn't crash. It didn't stumble. It just lowered. Quietly. Final.

A silent surrender.

I saw his eyes — not of a general, not even of a teacher — **but of a father, broken**. Searching the battlefield for something he could not name. His hand still held the bow. His armor still gleamed. But his heart... it was somewhere else.

And me? I stood there, hollow. Because in that one gesture — a floating chariot finding ground — I understood they had not just tricked a man. they had undone a legacy. Crossed into a space where victory no longer tasted like glory... only ash.

And when a warrior sets his weapons aside, **death is inevitable.**

Drishtadyumna, saw his moment. He struck.

The Acharya—my teacher, my commander and my strongest pillar—fell. Not by skill. Not by combat. But by deceit.

And yet, **they call us the unrighteous ones.**

Chapter 15
✦WORDS SHARPER THAN ARROWS✦

From the day I first became aware of my position in Hastinapura, Bhishma's towering presence loomed over me—not as a guide or a mentor, but as an unrelenting critic. He was the pillar of the Kuru dynasty, the grandsire whose words shaped the course of our lineage. And yet, for all his wisdom and supposed impartiality, his judgment of me was always steeped in disappointment, in disapproval that clung to me like a shadow.

I could see it in his eyes, hear it in the measured cadence of his voice. To Bhishma, I was not a rightful heir but a stubborn, arrogant prince consumed by my own ambition. He never saw the fire that drove me, the righteousness of my struggle.

No matter how hard I fought, how fiercely I defended my place, he regarded me as an obstacle rather than a leader.

It was no secret that Bhishma favored the Pandavas. He may have claimed neutrality, but his actions betrayed him.

Whenever Yudhishtira spoke, Bhishma listened with approval, as if the eldest Pandava alone carried the wisdom of kings.

Whenever Arjuna raised his bow, Bhishma's eyes shone with pride, as if no warrior could match his skill.

And yet, when I spoke of my vision for Hastinapura, Bhishma met me with silence or with words laced with veiled reprimand.

When I wielded my mace, no praise came forth—only reminders of how Balarama had trained both Bhima and me, as if to emphasize that I was not unique.

He clung to the ideals of dharma, yet refused to acknowledge the injustice that had been done to me. Was it Dharma that my birthright was constantly challenged?

Was it dharma that Yudhishtira, a man who gambled away his kingdom and his own wife, was deemed more virtuous than me? Bhishma never answered these questions.

He only insisted that I should bow to fate, that I should accept my place beneath the Pandavas, as if my very existence was an inconvenience to the order he so desperately sought to maintain.

Bhishma's words carried weight, not only within the palace but also among the noble houses that looked to Hastinapura for guidance. When he spoke against me, it was not just a matter of personal scorn—it undermined my authority.

His doubts fueled the skepticism of others, turning powerful allies into cautious bystanders.

His disapproval was never direct. No, Bhishma was far too careful for that. Instead, he would couch his criticism in the language of wisdom, in riddles of dharma that left me with no room to argue.

"A king must rule with righteousness, not with pride."
"A leader who does not listen to counsel walks a path of ruin."
"Strength alone does not make one worthy of a throne."

Each of these words was a blade, piercing through my resolve.

Yet, if he truly believed in dharma, why did he not stand against the Pandavas when they took what was mine? Why did he not speak when my father's love for me was questioned?

He was a man of great wisdom, but wisdom untempered by action is nothing more than empty philosophy.

It was Bhishma's insistence on fairness that led to my greatest struggles. He believed in peace, in diplomacy, in compromise. But the world is not built on compromise. It is built on strength, on decisive action. His refusal to take my side emboldened the Pandavas.

They knew that as long as Bhishma stood behind them, they could challenge me without fear of true consequence.

Even in war, he hesitated. As the commander of my army, I expected him to fight with the full might of the Kuru dynasty. And yet, he held back. He refused to harm the Pandavas in earnest, clinging to old affections instead of embracing his duty as a general.

What use was a warrior who would not strike? What use was a leader who would not commit fully to victory?

I tried to appeal to him, to remind him that his allegiance was to the throne of Hastinapura, not to five exiled princes.

But his heart had long been given to them. Perhaps it was guilt—guilt for his inaction when they were wronged in their youth, guilt for his failure to stop the division of the kingdom. Whatever the reason, that guilt made him weak.

And weakness, in war, is death.

In truth, Bhishma and I were never meant to see eye to eye. He was a relic of an era that had passed, a man bound by an oath that had long since lost its meaning. He believed in tradition, while I believed in forging my own path.

He spoke of dharma as if it were an unchanging law, but I saw it for what it was—a force that could be shaped, that could evolve with the times.

Perhaps, in another life, we could have been allies. If he had seen the world as I did, if he had recognized that I fought not out of arrogance but out of necessity, he might have been my greatest supporter. But that was not the path fate had chosen for us.

Bhishma stood against me not because I was wrong, but because he could not let go of the past. He could not see that the world was changing, that I was fighting to claim what was mine in a system that had always been stacked against me.

For all my anger, for all my frustration, there was still a part of me that longed for his approval.

I wanted Bhishma to see me as a worthy ruler, as a king who could lead Hastinapura into a new age. But that recognition never came.

When he lay dying on the bed of arrows, I looked at him one last time, searching for some sign that he understood me, that he saw beyond the image of the reckless prince he had painted in his mind.

But all he spoke of was dharma, of righteousness, of what should have been done. Even in his final moments, he could not bring himself to say that I was right.

And so, I turned away, carrying the weight of his judgment like a wound that would never heal.

Bhishma may have been a great warrior, a wise statesman, a legend in his own right. But to me, he was the one man who could have stood beside me, the one man whose support could have changed everything—yet he chose not to.

Chapter 16
✦THE SUN SETS IN BLOOD✦

The battlefield, once a glorious expanse of war cries and clashing steel, had begun to shrink. The earth drank the blood of warriors, the sky bore witness to the cries of the dying, and the sun, weary of the endless slaughter, hung low in the heavens, as if it, too, mourned the ruin of the Kuru dynasty.

I had lost much—my brothers, my soldiers, my kingdom hanging by a thread—but nothing had prepared me for the moment Karna fell.

The man who had stood beside me when the world called me unworthy. The man who had fought for me when Bhishma scorned me, when Dronacharya slighted me, when my name was whispered with disdain in the halls of Hastinapura.

My Karna, my shield, my truest friend—*was no more.*

I had known, in some unspoken part of my soul, that the war would claim him. We had both walked this path knowing there was no turning back. But knowing and witnessing are two different things.

When the news reached me, my heart clenched with a pain I had never known before.

I had lost brothers before, I had seen dear friends perish, but Karna... Karna was not just another warrior.

He was my strength, the only man who saw the world as I did. The only man who never judged me, never looked down upon me, never abandoned me even when the gods themselves conspired against us.

I could picture it clearly, as if I had been there: Karna standing tall in his chariot, his golden armor stripped away by the treachery of fate, his weapons still poised for battle. Arjuna before him, bow drawn, Krishna by his side, whispering words of war, of righteousness, of endings.

And then, that cruel stroke of fate—the chariot's wheel sinking into the earth, as if the gods themselves had reached out to bind him in shackles.

He had fought despite it, had struck Arjuna with a fury that could shake the heavens. But Krishna—always cunning, always scheming—knew this was his moment. He urged Arjuna forward, ignoring the rules of war, the dharma they so often preached when it suited them.

 A warrior was to be given a fair fight, but fairness had never been the way of the Pandavas.

And so, when Karna struggled, vulnerable for the first time, Krishna commanded Arjuna to shoot.

A coward's strike. A god's treachery.

And my greatest friend fell.

I felt the weight of his loss in my bones. The battlefield had become a graveyard, but it was Karna's death that truly buried me.

He was the sun that burned for my cause, the flame that kept my dream alive.

And now, **that sun had set.**

What did I have left? A dwindling army, warriors who once roared with confidence now whispering of fate and omens. The spirit of the Kauravas had always been tied to Karna's valor, to his undying belief that we could, and would, win. And with his fall, that belief cracked, like a dam that could no longer hold back the flood of doubt.

Shalya had led him into battle, but I had seen the disdain in his eyes, the reluctance in his hands. He was no ally. He did not fight for Karna, for me—he fought because he was bound by words, not loyalty. I should have been there. I should have ridden beside him, should have shielded him as he had shielded me a hundred times before.

But war does not care for should-haves. It only knows the language of death.

The irony did not escape me. Karna, the warrior who had been cursed by fate before he had even drawn his first breath.

Karna, who had given up his divine armor out of honor, only to be struck down when honor should have protected him. Karna, who had been denied by his own mother, abandoned by the very gods who had given him life.

Where was Krishna's dharma when Karna stood defenseless? Where was the justice the Pandavas so proudly preached?

The truth was bitter, but I had always known it: righteousness was a weapon wielded by the powerful. It was not an absolute truth, but a convenience, twisted and shaped by those who wished to justify their actions. Krishna, the man who claimed to uphold dharma, had broken it in the moment that mattered most.

And yet, they would sing songs of Arjuna's victory. They would call it fate, justice, the will of the gods.

I call it treachery.

I rode to where he had fallen, the battle forgotten for a fleeting moment. His lifeless body lay still on the ground, his face calm, almost at peace.

I had never seen Karna without his fire, without the unshakable will that had carried him through a life of injustice. Now, he was silent. Still.

The grief clawed at me, but I did not let it take me yet. I knelt beside him, my armor feeling heavier than ever before. *I did not cry. Not yet.* Instead, I traced my hand over the blood-stained soil beneath him, as if by some miracle, I could pull him back.

He had once told me that he was born to be on the battlefield, that his fate was to die with a weapon in his hand. **He had known**, long before any of us, that he was never meant to rule, never meant to sit upon a throne.

I had refused to believe it then. But now, I could not deny it.

He had fought not for himself, not for glory, but for me. For my cause. For the dream we had shared. And at that moment, as I looked at my fallen friend, I knew one thing above all—Karna had deserved better than this world had given him.

I rose to my feet, the battlefield suddenly feeling emptier than it had before. I still had warriors, still had weapons, still had a war to fight. But without Karna, *victory felt meaningless.*

The Pandavas had taken much from me, but this—this was unforgivable. If they thought I would falter, they were wrong.

Karna had fought until his last breath, and I would do the same. If they wanted my throne, **they would have to take it from my lifeless hands.**

Karna was gone. The one man who stood beside me not out of blood, not out of duty, but out of sheer loyalty—struck down by treachery. My world had already begun to collapse, yet fate was not done with me. Now, it came for the man who had started it all.

Shakuni.

The master of the game. The architect of destruction. The one who had set every piece into motion—cut down by the very war he had unleashed.

Sahadeva, with vengeance in his eyes, struck him down without hesitation. There was no plea, no resistance.

Shakuni did not beg, nor did he falter. He met death the way he had met life—with calculation, with cold acceptance, with the knowledge that his work was done.

But did he have to die like this?

A part of me shattered at the sight. He was my uncle—**my Mama**. The man who had whispered my first tales of war, who had guided my hand in the games of strategy. The man who had taught me how to dream of a throne, how to fight for what was rightfully mine.

And yet, here he was—lifeless, unmoving, his sharp mind silenced forever.

I wanted to call out to him. To demand that he wake up, that he look at me one last time, that he speak—just one word, just one final lesson.

But there was nothing.

For all his wit, for all his cunning, even Shakuni could not outplay death.

I stood there, frozen, unable to accept that he was gone. Had he seen this moment in his mind long before the first dice was cast? Had he known that when the last move had been played, he too would be a piece sacrificed to the board?

Perhaps he did.

For he had never fought for a crown. Never for glory. Never for me.

He fought for his father. For his clan. For his own vengeance.

And in that, **he had won.**

His body lay lifeless, but his victory was eternal—Hastinapura was in ruin, the Kuru name bathed in the blood of its own sons. The kingdom that had wronged him was gone.

And so was he.

Was this what he had wanted?

To see the empire crumble under the weight of its own sins? To watch the Kuru bloodline stain the very soil it ruled?

If it was, then Shakuni had been the greatest player of us all. Not even Krishna, with all his wisdom and divine machinations, could have orchestrated a destruction as complete as this.

But he had played his final move.

And now, he was gone.

Mama was the only one who had never abandoned me.
Even when the world turned against me, even when my own brothers fell into doubt, he had stayed.

And now, fate had taken him too.

I wanted to scream at the heavens, to demand why the gods let him fall. Why they let Karna fall. Why they let everything I held dear slip through my fingers like sand.

I turned away, unable to look at him any longer. The man who had promised to destroy the Kuru dynasty had done exactly that. No hesitation. No partiality.

Not even for me.

I turned away from his body, my grief buried deep within the walls of my heart. There would be time for mourning when the war was over. For now, I had only one purpose left.

To finish what we started.

To make the Pandavas pay.

Chapter 17
✦GLORY AND GRAVE✦

The battlefield of Kurukshetra, once alive with the clash of swords and the cries of warriors, had now fallen into an eerie silence. The earth, drenched in the blood of countless soldiers, bore the scars of a war that had devoured everything in its path. What had begun as a battle for dharma had now reduced the great kingdom of Kuru to ashes. My brothers, my warriors, my closest friends—everyone who had stood by me had fallen.

I, Duryodhana, the son of Dhritarashtra, the rightful heir of Hastinapura, stood alone. But even in my solitude, I refused to bend. A Kshatriya does not cower before fate; he meets it with open arms.

I had lost my kingdom. But I had not yet lost myself.

Exhausted and wounded, I sought refuge in the still waters of Dwaipayana Lake. The cool embrace of the lake soothed my battle-worn body, offering me a fleeting respite from the weight of my losses. The water cleansed the dirt and blood from my skin, but it could not wash away the burden of betrayal that had brought me here.

Everything had been taken from me—my father sat blind in his palace, helpless and broken, my mother's silent prayers had done nothing to alter destiny, and my warriors had perished, their loyalty repaid with death. Karna, my dearest friend and truest ally, had fallen to treachery.

Even the mighty Bhishma and Dronacharya, whom I had revered, had been struck down by deceit.

And yet, in the wake of such devastation, the Pandavas had the audacity to claim they fought for righteousness.

A bitter smile crossed my lips. What righteousness was this, where honor was shattered and dharma was nothing but a weapon wielded for victory?

If Krishna, the divine protector of dharma, had to rely on cunning and trickery to secure the Pandavas' triumph, then was it truly dharma that had won? Or had deception merely disguised itself as a virtue?

I closed my eyes, letting the water cool my fevered mind. If fate had decreed my end, then let it come. But let it come in battle, not in hiding.

It was not long before they arrived.

Standing at the shore, the five brothers glared down at me, their faces unreadable in the dying light. Beside them stood Krishna, his ever-knowing gaze fixed upon me.

It was he who spoke first, his voice smooth and unshaken, as if he had foreseen this moment long before it had come to pass.

Yudhishtira, the so-called embodiment of dharma, stepped forward, his words laced with a false magnanimity.

He called for me to emerge and fight my final battle. He promised that if I defeated one of them in single combat, the kingdom would be mine.

I could not contain the laughter that rose from my throat. How easy it was for them to speak of fairness now, when their victory had already been sealed by treachery.

Where was this righteousness when Karna was struck down in a moment of helplessness?

Where was their code of honor when Abhimanyu was slain by an army? Where was their dharma when Shikhandi was sent to attack Bhishma?

But I did not voice these thoughts. I merely rose from the waters, feeling the weight of my battered body, yet standing tall. If they sought to see me broken, they would be disappointed. I would fight. Not for the kingdom, not for victory, but because I was a warrior, and a warrior's duty is to meet his fate with dignity.

Bhima stepped forward. I had known it would be him. Of all the Pandavas, it was he who hated me most.

From childhood, he had burned with the desire to see me fall. Today, he would have his chance.

The war had left us both weary, but I had trained my body for years, forged in the discipline of the mace. My blows were precise, calculated. Bhima fought with brute force, his rage driving his strikes, but I met him evenly. Each clash of our maces sent shockwaves through the ground, the dust rising like specters of the warriors who had already fallen.

With each strike, I could see the frustration in his eyes. He had thought me weak, that my wounds and despair would make me easy to defeat. But I was Duryodhana, the son of the Kuru dynasty. I had trained under Balarama himself, and there was no one who could best me in this art.

I fought not for victory, but for honor. If I was to fall, it would be through strength, not deceit.

And then, the tide shifted—not by skill, but by treachery.

From the corner of my vision, I saw Krishna lean toward Bhima, his voice a whisper of poison. I did not hear the words, but I knew what had been said the moment Bhima's stance changed.

He lunged again, but this time, his target was not my head, not my torso—no, he struck lower. His mace came crashing down upon my thighs, shattering the bones beneath.

I did not cry out. I would not give them that satisfaction. But the agony was indescribable. My legs, once the foundation of my power, had been destroyed by a single cowardly strike. The ground rushed to meet me as I collapsed, my weapon slipping from my fingers.

I had been deceived.

Bhima had broken the very rule of combat that we had sworn to uphold. A mace duel was to be fought with honor—no blows below the waist, no unfair strikes. Yet Krishna, the so-called protector of dharma, had guided his champion's hand in betrayal.

I laughed—short, sharp, bitter. The taste of blood filled my mouth, but I did not care.

The Pandavas had won their war, but in doing so, they had proved themselves no better than me.

So this was their dharma.

As I lay on the ground, the pain numbing my senses, I looked up at the sky. The same sky that had once stretched over my kingdom, the same sky that had witnessed my rise, now bore witness to my fall.

The Pandavas stood over me, their faces alight with victory, yet I saw something else—uncertainty.

Perhaps they had expected me to weep, to curse them, to beg for mercy. But I did none of these things.

I had lost everything, but I had not lost myself.

I turned my gaze to Krishna, the architect of my defeat. He watched me with that inscrutable expression, as if he had foreseen this moment long before it came. Perhaps he had. Perhaps the gods had already written this end into the stars.

But even if I was to die, I would die knowing one truth.

I had fought with honor. They had won through deception.

History would call them victors, but I knew better. In their hearts, they would always remember—**Duryodhana did not fall.**

He was struck down.

The war was over, the sun had set, and with it, so had my kingdom, my dreams, my very being. But even as life ebbed away, my mind refused to be silent. It drifted back to the betrayal that had sealed my fate before I even stepped onto the battlefield.

Krishna.

I had always known him to be my opponent, the ever-smiling architect of the Pandavas' victories. But never had his cunning struck so cruelly as it did that day in my mother's chamber.

Gandhari, my mother—blindfolded by choice, yet never blind to my suffering—had called for me. She had wished to bless me, to make my body invincible with the strength of her unwavering austerities.

Every day of her life, she had denied herself sight, and every moment of mine had been a battle against fate.

And so, she had asked me to come before her **unclothed**, that she may finally see me, for the first and last time, and fortify my flesh against the weapons of my enemies.

I had obeyed. Or rather, I had intended to.

Until Krishna.

He had found me on my way, that ever-knowing gaze piercing through me like an arrow. And with his honeyed words, he had placed doubt in my heart.

"A prince, walking naked through his palace? Have you no shame, Duryodhana?"

Shame?

Krishna's words slithered into my mind, whispering, mocking, and planting hesitation where there was none.

And so, I wrapped myself in a cloth—just a simple piece of fabric around my waist, nothing more.

But when my mother removed her blindfold and saw me, standing not in complete bareness but covered, her face fell. A flicker of sorrow passed through her, so quick, so fleeting, I almost missed it.

"Why did you not trust me, my son?" she had whispered.

She did not say more. She simply raised her hands and let her blessings flow.

And just like that, the invincibility she had wished to grant me was incomplete.

My thighs remained unprotected.

And now, here I was, lying upon the battlefield, struck down by Bhima's cruel mace *exactly where Krishna had ensured I would be weak.*

It had never been just war.

It had been a game—a game where I was but a piece to be moved, deceived, and sacrificed.

And Krishna?

He had played it to perfection.

Pain coursed through my body like fire, when my thigh was shattered by Bhima's treacherous blow. My vision blurred, but my mind remained sharp.

I knew I was dying. But not as a fallen man. Not as a coward.

I could accept the pain. I could even accept defeat. But what I could never accept—**was dishonor.**

Bhima stood before me, his chest heaving, his eyes alight with savage triumph. And then, in an act more vile than the blow itself, he danced.

A grotesque, mocking gyration, his massive form swaying in exaggerated victory, his laughter echoing across the battlefield. My fingers dug into the earth beneath me.

Was this the great dharma of the Pandavas?

Was this nobility?

Was this righteousness?

And then, Krishna spoke.

"Bhima, enough. This is not the way of dharma. A true warrior does not dishonor his fallen enemy."

I let out a slow breath, a bitter smile tugging at my lips. Dharma? Now, he speaks of dharma?

Where was this dharma Bhima struck me below the waist, breaking the very laws of battle that Krishna himself had preached?

And now, he wished to preserve their honor?

No. They would hear the truth before I left this world.

I raised my head, my voice hoarse but unwavering. "Tell me, cousins, who among us has lived a greater life?"

I let my words settle, watching as the weight of them sank into their very bones.

"The pandavas, who spent years in exile, torn away from their home, walking a path not of their choosing? Or I, who built and ruled a kingdom, who lived with the power to shape my own destiny?"

Bhima's smirk faltered. Arjuna looked away. Good. Let them listen.

I drew a ragged breath and let out a bitter chuckle. "And tell me, **brothers**, who among us has earned a more fitting end?"

I gestured weakly around me. "I die here, on the battlefield, under the open sky, surrounded by warriors. I fall as a Kshatriya should, with my weapon in hand and my duty fulfilled. There is no shame in my end."

I closed my eyes briefly, feeling the cold touch of fate pressing upon me.

"The war is over, and they stand victorious. But when the weapons are laid to rest, when the blood has dried and when the echoes of battle fade into silence... **will they truly find peace?**"

I exhaled, a slow, steady breath.

"I do not leave this world defeated. I leave knowing I lived as I willed, fought as I must, and fell as befits a warrior."

Silence.

The wind carried away the last whispers of battle. The sky, vast and endless, bore witness to my fall.

And as the cold earth welcomed me into its embrace, I let out one final breath. Not of regret.

But of defiance.

Chapter 18
✦IN THE COURT OF TIME AND TRUTH✦

And so, I have spoken.

From the echoes of Hastinapura's corridors to the blood-soaked fields of Kurukshetra, I have laid bare the truth as I lived it.

Not as the poets have sung, not as the victors have proclaimed, but as it was—through my eyes, through my heart. I have spared no detail, no failure, no triumph. I have given you my truth, my dharma.

Now, the weight of silence settles around me, heavier than the mace that once rested in my hands.

Before me, Yama sits unmoved, his expression unreadable. The divine judge, the keeper of fate, the one who will decide what remains of me beyond this moment. But he has listened. I know he has. That is all I asked. That is all I ever wanted.

When I arrived in this realm, broken and weary, I had demanded one thing—not mercy, not absolution, but a hearing.

I had seen how history was shaped by the voices of victors, how those who lost were buried not just in earth but in shame, in silence. I refused to be silent.

And so I told him everything.

How I was never the monster they painted me to be. How I was a prince, a brother, a friend.

How I was born into a world that had already cast its judgment upon me. How I fought, not for greed or vengeance, but for my right.

For my father, my brothers and my kingdom. How I was betrayed, not by fate, but by those who claimed to be righteous.

How I lost—everything, everyone—and yet, even in defeat, I refused to kneel.

I told him of my pride, my missteps, my arrogance. I did not hide my flaws. I own them, just as I own my virtues.

I was not perfect.

But neither were those who condemned me.

The silence stretches longer.

I wonder if the souls who have heard my tale have begun to question their own beliefs.

If the mighty Bhishma, wherever he rests, still clings to his notions of dharma, or if he now sees the cracks in the righteousness he upheld.

If Yudhishtira, upon his throne of virtue, ever wakes in the night and wonders whether his truth was the only truth.

If Krishna—yes, even Krishna—acknowledges, somewhere in the vastness of the universe, that I was not wrong in everything. That my war was not without reason.

Yama's gaze remains steady. He will speak soon, I know. He will tell me my fate. But at this moment, I feel no fear.

I have stood before death, faced the cruelty of fate, endured the judgment of the world.

What can he say that I have not already lived?

I am Duryodhana.

Not a demon. Not a saint.

I was a warrior. A king. A man.

And now, my story is told.

Let judgment come.

EPILOGUE

Darkness stretches before me, vast and endless. I do not know if this is the end or the beginning. Perhaps it is both.

I have spoken. I have torn open the past, laid my soul bare before Yama, before the gods, before those who have always judged me without ever knowing me. The war is over. The victors have sung their songs. The world remembers what it chooses to remember. But I—I have carved my truth into eternity.

And yet, what does it matter?

I lost everything. My brothers—my flesh and blood—lie as bones on the fields of Kurukshetra. My father, who spent his life in darkness, lived only to see his lineage destroyed. My mother—ah, my mother—she loved me, but she could never fight for me. My friend, my Karna, the one soul who stood beside me when all others turned away, is gone.

Slain by trickery, abandoned by fate, his body left to burn beneath the very sun he worshipped.

What remains of me now?

They call me arrogant. They say I was blinded by pride. But was it pride to fight for what was mine? Was it arrogance to refuse to kneel before those who had wronged me? Was it truly *adharma* to love my friend beyond caste, beyond fate, beyond the whispers of the world?

I was not perfect. I was not gentle, nor forgiving, nor meek. I did not bend like Yudhishtira, I did not bow like Bhishma. I was fire and steel, a man who was never meant to surrender.

But they will never understand what it was to be me.

To be born into a world that had already cast its judgment. To hear, even as a child, the murmurs that I was undeserving.

To watch the elders of my house—the so-called guardians of dharma—favor the sons of another over me, the rightful heir.

To fight, not just for a throne, but for my very existence.

And in the end, I lost.

Or did I?

I look at Yama, his eyes deep and ancient, weighing my soul, deciding my fate. Heaven will not open its doors for me. The world of the gods is not for men like me.

They will welcome Yudhishtira, seat him among the righteous, shower him with garlands for upholding a dharma that was never questioned. They will embrace Arjuna, Krishna's beloved, the hero of their tale. Even Karna—my Karna—will find his place among them, for he was the son of the sun god, touched by divinity.

But I—I was mortal. *Only* mortal.

Perhaps they will cast me into the darkness, into the fire of punishment they reserve for men they deem unworthy. Perhaps my soul will wander forever, denied rest, denied peace.

But I am not afraid.

Because I know this much—my name will never fade. They will curse it, they will spit upon it, they will call me the villain, the tyrant, the unrighteous king.

But they will *remember* me.

And if, centuries from now, a single soul hears my story and wonders—*was he truly so wrong?*—then I have won.

I was not the hero of this tale. I was not meant to be.

But I was never the monster they painted me to be, either.

I was Duryodhana. A prince, a warrior, a man who dared to fight. A man who stood, even when the world pushed him down.

And I will stand still, even in the afterlife.

Let Yama speak his judgment. Let fate do as it will.

I am ready.

APPENDICES

Appendix I: The Characters Reimagined

This retelling of the *Mahabharata* through Duryodhana's perspective presents familiar characters in a new light. Below is a brief overview of their roles as they appear in this narrative:

- **Duryodhana** – The central figure of this retelling, Duryodhana is portrayed not as a ruthless villain, but as a flawed, ambitious, and fiercely loyal prince fighting for his rightful claim. His actions stem from deep-seated grievances and his belief in justice as he perceives it.

- **Karna** – The one true friend Duryodhana trusts above all. A warrior cast aside by fate, Karna's struggles mirror Duryodhana's own. His loyalty remains unshaken, making his loss the most personal tragedy of all.

- **Shakuni** – A master strategist and Duryodhana's greatest influence. His hatred for the Kuru dynasty fuels his actions, often blurring the line between guidance and manipulation.

- **Bhishma** – The grandsire of the Kuru dynasty, an enigma to Duryodhana. Though revered as a protector, he stands in the way of Duryodhana's dreams, questioning his every move.

- **Krishna** – A force of destiny, forever opposed to Duryodhana. Though wise and divine, his role in the destruction of the Kauravas leaves Duryodhana questioning the nature of righteousness.

- **The Pandavas** – The rivals who shaped Duryodhana's life. Their actions, viewed from his perspective, appear less virtuous, raising questions about their claim to dharma.

- **Draupadi** – A woman wronged, yet also a symbol of defiance. Her role in the conflict is seen through the lens of a man who underestimated the consequences of his own actions.

Appendix II: The Concept of Dharma in This Narrative

Dharma, the moral and ethical law governing the universe, is at the heart of the *Mahabharata*. However, as this story reveals, dharma is not a singular, universal truth—it shifts based on perspective.

- **Duryodhana's Dharma** – He believes in the right to rule, in the strength of his will, and in the loyalty of those who stand by him. To him, denying the Pandavas their claim is not injustice but an assertion of his rightful inheritance.

- **Krishna's Dharma** – He serves the greater cosmic order, ensuring that dharma prevails, even at the cost of deception, war, and destruction.

- **Bhishma's Dharma** – A vow-bound duty to the throne, despite witnessing injustice, leaving him torn between honor and morality.

- **Karna's Dharma** – A struggle between loyalty to his friend and the truth of his birth, forcing him to choose between love and righteousness.

THEMES AND MOTIFS

The Duality of Dharma – Morality is not absolute; what is just can change based on perspective.

The Burden of Legacy – Inheritance and societal expectations shape a person's destiny and struggles.

The Complexity of Good and Evil – There are no true heroes or villains; every action has its justification.

Friendship and Loyalty – Bonds formed beyond birth and fate can define a person's choices and downfall.

The Weight of Choices – Every decision carries consequences, but was it a personal choice or cosmic design?

Fate vs. Free Will – Do individuals shape their own destiny, or is everything preordained?

The Role of Women – Women are not just bystanders; they influence war, power, and fate in crucial ways.

Mortals vs. Gods – The struggle between human will and divine intervention shapes the course of history.

The Cost of War – War does not distinguish between right and wrong; it only leaves destruction behind.

Redemption and Judgment – A single life is a sum of its deeds, but who decides what is truly righteous.

SPECIAL THANKS

To my father, Prabhu and grandfather, Mohanan—your stories of our culture shaped my imagination and led me to this moment.

To my mother, Uma—your unwavering belief and encouragement made this journey possible.

To my sister, A.P—you helped shape the person I am today. This book belongs to you as much as it does to me.

To my illustrator, Joshua—for illustrating my book and designing my book cover so beautifully. Your artistry has truly brought my vision to life, and I am forever grateful for your dedication and talent.

To Madhuri Ma'am and Renju Ma'am—thank you for motivating me and pushing me forward every time I felt like giving up.

To Anagha, C.S and Purvi—thank you for your suggestions and for always being by my side as I struggled. Your support meant the world to me.

Last but not least,

To my readers—thank you for stepping into this world with me and making this story your own.

ABOUT THE AUTHOR

Nivasini is a 17-year-old author and self-publisher from Chennai, Tamil Nadu. She studied at Maharishi Vidya Mandir, Hyderabad, and successfully published her debut book while still in Grade 12. From a young age, Nivasini has been profoundly drawn to Indian mythology and the art of storytelling. Growing up in a home where rich tales of gods, goddesses, and epic sagas were regularly shared by her father and grandfather, she developed a deep connection to the cultural roots and traditions of her heritage. These stories, often steeped in wisdom, history, and divine teachings, not only shaped her understanding of dharma but also revealed the intricate layers of truth that lie beyond the surface of everyday life. Her passion for these timeless narratives has inspired her to write and share stories that honor and preserve the essence of Indian mythology.

DURYODHANA: The Other Side Of The Mahabharata is her debut novel, a bold reimagining of one of the Mahabharata's most misunderstood warriors. More than just a story, this book is a tribute to her father and grandfather, whose stories ignited her passion for mythology and inspired her journey as a writer.

When she isn't lost in the world of ancient tales, Nivasini enjoys reading, researching historical texts, and exploring the philosophical depths of storytelling. She believes that every legend has multiple sides—and that the other side often holds a story worth telling.